THE

COMPASS™

ALSO BY TAMMY KLING

Exit Row

There's More to Life Than the Corner Office

Transform from where you are, to where you want to be.

THE COMPASS™

TAMMY KLING • JOHN SPENCER ELLIS

Vanguard Press
A Member of the Perseus Books Group

Published by Vanguard Press
A Member of the Perseus Books Group

Designed by Jill Shaffer
Set in 12 point Sabon by Eclipse Publishing Services

Cataloging-in-Publication data for this book is available from the
Library of Congress.
ISBN 13: 978-1-59315-561-2

Vanguard Press books are available at special discounts for bulk
purchases in the U.S. by corporations, institutions, and other
organizations. For more information, please contact the Special Markets
Department at the Perseus Books Group, 2300 Chestnut Street,
Suite 200, Philadelphia, PA 19103, or call (800) 810-4145, ext. 5000,
or e-mail special.markets@perseusbooks.com.

10 9 8 7 6 5 4 3 2 1

For Mark, Reed, and Luke

CONTENTS

ACKNOWLEDGMENTS

We'd like to thank the fabulous team at Perseus for their dedication and love for this book. Roger, Amanda, and Georgina, you're the best! Thanks to Peter Miller at PMA for being a fantastic manager, and to Adrienne for her love of literary excellence and guidance! Finally, thanks to our loved ones and to the One who made this book possible, the inspiration for it all.

Chapter 1

NIGHT

*Sometimes you must let go of the life
you had planned in order to make room
for the life ahead of you.*

Five seconds can alter your life forever. It can change the course of your dreams and wipe out everything you'd ever hoped for. It can send you into the wilderness, in search of nothing.

✳

Three days into the Nevada desert I felt the soles of my shoes melting. I stopped, turned one foot upside down, and examined the bottom of my sneaker. The rubber fibers seemed to be on fire, heating to higher temperatures with each step.

Waves of heat rose off of the surface of the red sands. It was miles outside of Amargosa near Death Valley, the driest place on earth. I didn't know when I'd find nourishment, and I didn't care.

I knew from my research in neurobiology that the brain could last several days without water. The dendrites would repair themselves; the synapses would still fire. The brain was an amazing organ with the ability to repair itself against even the worst circumstances. But if I didn't find water soon, dehydration would set in, and *my* brain could lapse into confusion. I'd start seeing things, hearing things . . .

I took a step forward through an arroyo, scanning the landscape for a cactus. Inside would be gallons of water, and some species had sustained the lives of ancient Indian tribes wandering the desert for years. I walked for another five minutes until I found a craggy rock and sat down, lowering my head into the palm of my hands.

I had no plan and no desire for one. When I'd started out, I had wanted only to escape.

※

Before I had set out on my journey, they'd insisted on throwing a small farewell gathering for me, and, amidst the chaos, I heard something muttered from the back of the room.

"It's almost as if his life has been divided into two sections: *before the accident and after.*"

It was true. I was a different man now. I felt like a cadaver divided down the middle with a Stryker saw, my breastbone cut open, exposing the organs. Like a body during an autopsy, my heart had been ripped out and placed on top of my chest for examination. The blood had ceased to flow. I *was* a cadaver.

Hollow.

※

I considered eating the small energy bar I had left in my backpack, but I knew that if I did there was a chance it would make things worse. My insides would tighten. Water was needed for digestion, and the food wouldn't get through the small intestine without it.

"You okay?"

The voice startled me, and I looked up into the sun. I rubbed my eyes and swallowed hard, my throat parched and sore.

Was the process beginning?

"Here's some water if you need it." The voice was gruff, yet distinctly female. Through the glare I saw that she had graying hair and a creviced jaw darkened with lines. She held the slim canteen toward me. "The waters hot, but it's better than nothing. Only a fool comes out here without a canteen."

I took it and unscrewed the metal top, downing it.

"You lost?" she asked.

I shook my head, "No."

"No one sane comes this far," she said. "Must be lost. In one way or another."

The woman wore brown shorts and a long-sleeved cotton shirt with pockets and snaps down the front and on the arms. A large black camera hung from a leather strap around her neck. She kicked at the dirt with her boots to make a small clearing, something I'd once read about in a desert manual. Experienced trail guides did it to check for scorpions and rattlers before they sat down.

"You got a name?" she asked.

I held the canteen a little longer, considered drinking, then wondered if it was all she had.

"Jonathan," I said. "Jonathan Taylor."

"Jonathan, do you realize that it's 115 degrees out here?"

I said nothing and shrugged.

"You need more than a t-shirt," she continued. "And jeans aren't the best thing for the desert.

"I've got a tent over there," she said, pointing to a small clearing of trees. She tapped the camera. "You can rest in the shade as long as you want. I'm here for a week, taking pictures." She looked intently at my face. "You've got a bad wound there. You need something for it?"

I touched the left side of my jaw. It had been two months now, but the wound wouldn't heal. I shook my head.

"I'm fine."

"You don't look fine," she replied.

"So why are you *here*?" I asked. "Why the desert? It's pretty desolate out here, and there's not much to see."

"I'm a psychologist," she said. "Former, that is. Always wanted to be a photographer, but it's the one dream I never fulfilled. I've always loved the open space of the desert, and I guess you could say I've escaped my life to come to this place. To shoot my last photos."

"Your last?" I looked at her curiously.

"I'm dying," she said matter-of-factly.

"Aren't we all?" I replied.

As soon as I said it, I wished I could take it back.

I looked at her dark expression and knew it was true. She really was dying.

"I'm sorry," I whispered.

The woman just laughed.

"Don't be. It's not about being sorry. We all have a beginning, and we all have an end."

"But is there a cure? What's wrong with you?"

"I have cancer, and it's terminal," she said flatly. "Ironically, it's a brain tumor. Imagine that, a psychologist who uses her brain all her life, with a brain tumor. There is no cure. But it's okay, Jonathan. I've made peace with it. I've chosen to come here." She turned to look straight at me. "And you?"

"I flew in and just started walking. I walked for days, slept outside. That's about it. I ended up here kinda by accident."

She pondered that for a moment, then stood and took the canteen from my hand.

"There are no accidents," she said, motioning me to follow. "We may think that there are, but there aren't. You have a family?"

I stood and walked slowly, following her toward the tree clearing where she had set up camp, and pondered the irony of her words.

There are no accidents.

What the hell? I thought about my wife and daughter. *Yes,* I said silently. *There are accidents.*

"See, I'm taking photos of that rock outcropping as the sun sets," the woman said, pointing to a distant canyon. The mountain range was wide and distinct, with tall peaks jutting high into the heavens. "It's very different from the kind of work I've done my whole life. I've found my passion now. I've discovered my destiny. I may not have more than a few weeks to live it, but that's not important." She sounded sincere.

"What kind of work did you do in psychology?"

"Hemispheric integration."

"Hemispheric what?"

"I helped people understand the wide capacity of their minds."

"My wife was a first-year neurologist," I said. "But I've never heard that term."

"Was?"

I looked down into the brown sand.

"Was," I said firmly.

"Well, when we experience an event in our lives," the woman explained, "we record in our memory two separate and unique pictorial representations—one in each of the brain's hemispheres. The left hemisphere is responsible for logical, linear thinking. The right is more concerned with spatial relationships and concepts such as personal safety."

"And?" I replied, intrigued.

"And if we consistently use the perception from only one side of the brain, our choices are limited, and personal issues remain unresolved. Learning conscious control over which hemispheric image to utilize broadens our range of choices, and more responses become available to us. Imagine being able to understand and access the brain as it was designed to be used.

"Accessing this second hemisphere opens doors that we didn't even know existed."

I shrugged.

I wondered if there was some way I could change my own way of thinking, reprogram my brain to see the events of the past one hundred days entirely differently. If I could drive by that intersection just one more time and experience nothing—instead of seeing the image of them lying in the road, that last breath . . .

Maybe my life could change.

Maybe I could rewind, go back to the old job, go back to the house, back to the former friends, and act as if life were just a series of peaks and valleys. Maybe I would be able to overcome the valley. Get remarried. Be like the others in our society who are so good at reincarnating, adopting second lives.

I could have a whole new wife, a new kid, and justify it all by saying *there are no accidents*, and reach the understanding that it was destined to be. Feel as if I were destined to be with this new person, destined to bring another life into this world. Ignore the fact that the first family ever existed and got wiped away in a single moment.

Problem was, I could see none of it. I was hollow.

"Why didn't you jump?" she asked.

I looked at her blankly.

"You wanted to jump," she continued. "You wanted to end it all at the overpass, at that intersection, and join your little girl on the other side. You thought that would ease your pain. What stopped you?"

"I didn't tell you that," I said.

"But it's true."

The intersection seemed to be a metaphor for my life. There was an intersection at the end of the road, and I had to make a decision. Would I turn left? Or would it be right? There was nowhere else to go. I had stood there on the pavement in the days following the accident, like an eggshell, crumbling. I stood at the side of the overpass and clung to the railing, vomiting in the rain.

I had removed my coat. Puddles seeped into my sneakers, but I didn't care. I took them off, stood barefoot in the middle of a torrential downpour and wailed. I shouted at the top of my lungs, cursing at Lacy and God and anyone who would listen, as my heart emptied and everything was replaced with rage.

I don't know how long I'd been there or how I made it out. The overpass was a short walk from the impact site, and the bottom was more than twenty feet down, with rocks below.

I hadn't told her about that moment. I hadn't told anyone.

"Who are you?" I asked, feeling anger rising inside my gut. "Are you a psychic or something? One of those witches who can see into someone's life?"

The woman laughed.

"I'm not a witch," she said. "But who are *you*?"

✳

The road that Lacy and Boo had been on was the kind of road that went on for ages. Not miles, nor minutes, nor hours, but it seemed as if there were no exits, no roadside diners, or interruptions—just one intersection three miles from our tiny house. Before the accident, there were times I drove that road just listening to the hum of the engine, with no radio or cell phone to distract me. Years ago someone had nicknamed it the *forever highway* because it wound through cornfields from one end out west to the other, connecting a whole string of states. It snaked up into the mountains and down to the sea. It wound through California into the flat red sands, and it wound so tightly around my family at that intersection that day that it squeezed the life out.

Years before the accident, I recall driving in the dark of night, wondering what would happen if my car broke down and how I'd make it back. I'd have to get out to walk, in search of a service station. Maybe another traveler would come along and find remnants of my bones and go on, or maybe I'd be carried away by vultures.

"What's your name?" I asked. They were the only words I could manage.

"Marilyn," she said warmly.

I glanced at her profile, noticing a small drop of sweat traveling down her throat. She had a death sentence, yet she seemed more centered than I'd *ever* been, as if she had a built-in compass of some sort that had guided her all her life. Here she was, an old woman in the middle of the desert, yet completely at home.

"Could there be any other meaning to this?" I asked. "You think there's a reason we're sitting here in the center of this scorched earth, in the middle of October? Just the two of us poor pitiful souls?"

She began laughing again then. She threw back her head, and, to my surprise, I laughed, too, for the first time since the accident. I leaned against the nearest tree and felt a sharp layer of bark against my flesh and a rush of strength and adrenaline. It felt good to feel *something*. I laughed hard, pulled out of my numbness, until I began to cry.

The tears fell and my body heaved with sobs.

"I don't know why I'm here," I admitted, gasping for air and wiping my face with my arm. "I don't know what I'm seeking . . . "

"Does anyone?" she asked.

"I don't know . . . "

I had a flashback then. Boo in her car seat with a pink plastic sippy cup in the cup holder. "I want my bear," Boo said, pointing to the stuffed animal on the ground. It had tumbled out of the Explorer onto the driveway when we opened the door.

I should have turned back then. I should have stopped everything and seen it as a sign to halt.

Stop.

Don't let them go.

"Get it," Boo said, like a demanding little dictator. As always, I relented and picked it up, handed it to her, and kissed her on her cheek.

"I love you, daddy," she said, beaming.

※

The woman in the desert looked at me and waited for my thoughts to leave.

"Jonathan, none of us knows anything. We *think* we know, then it turns out that we don't. The universe has a way of intervening. Of changing you. In the end, you don't know what you're seeking, and you don't know what you'll find."

I shook my head, baffled.

"But it's all irrelevant, anyway," she said. "Because it doesn't matter what you seek or what you find. What matters is that you allow your compass to guide you, and let your gifts and knowledge rise to the surface, so you can live out your life's purpose." She thought for a moment.

"It's worth the journey," she said.

Chapter 2

ESCAPE

*"This path we were forced to take as best we might,
in single file, and there I was—the flames to
the left of me, and the abyss to the right."*

— DANTE ALIGHIERI

There are moments in your life that change the course of your destiny forever.

Some people like me, have already had them. Others have not, but that moment is ahead, like a shark that prowls the ocean floor.

We are merely helpless swimmers on the surface above, thinking we're in control and seeing only the shore in the distance. For most people, it's worth swimming toward, worth fighting for. The shore provides hope, the horizon above it an entrance into a new world.

We swim, achieve, work hard, and all the while keep moving toward the future.

Yet what lies beneath is everything because it has the power to change your world, envelop you in darkness, and alter everything you thought you believed.

After the accident, I remember thinking of a different analogy—of the mind as a battlefield. It was three days into *detention* as I called it, a place my family had checked me into to save me from myself. It was an intake facility in Tucson, where the counselors treated me with drugs for depression and daily doses of therapy. The tables were littered with books that boasted intentionally uplifting titles.

They tried to heal the wound on my jaw, but it refused to cooperate.

It was different from the therapist they had sent me to in California. There were different ways of pulling things out of you. I had been driven to Tucson by my brother, and I remained for a few days, talked it out, and then escaped a month before he was due to pick me up again. I rode a Greyhound back home and went in to work the next day as if nothing had happened.

On the bus ride I discovered a newspaper in the seat, a headline about a woman who had opened the door of an airplane in mid-flight and jumped. They found her body in a field of flowers with a note still tucked in her suit pocket.

It is on this day, she had written, *that I have lost all hope.*

I tore the article out and kept her picture in my pocket for months. Blonde, red cherub cheeks, a smile of sunshine and daisies, like the field they had found her in. The face of hope.

On the day I left suburbia for the desert, I had no illusions that I'd ever return. On that day, all hope was lost. I'd exhausted all of my options. Worked without working. Slept without sleeping. Talked without remembering what I'd said or to whom I'd said it.

✳

"So what's next on your journey?" Marilyn asked. She pulled a music device that looked like an iPod from her pocket and untangled the cord.

The morning sun rose over the mountains behind her.

I lifted my arms toward the sky, stretching them wide. I gauged my feelings, as I had become accustomed to doing. In grief therapy, the psychotherapist who tried to crack open my skull and pour sunshine in had outlined the stages of mourning, and they were fixed there forever. One tool was to get your body moving, even if it was something small, like stretching. In the mornings I thought through all of those grief stages without even trying to.

Sadness, anger, despair, forgiveness.

I was stuck in the first three without any hope of achieving the last one. Each morning it was despair, pure and black. The Darkness that defined my life now was etched into my soul.

It's almost as if his life has been divided into two sections: before the accident and after.

✳

"Did I sleep?" I asked. I didn't attempt a smile.

She nodded that indeed I had, and it was for the first time in months that I had done so without meds.

"You snored a little," she said. "It was a deep REM sleep." She put the earbuds into her ears and turned on the device.

✳

The world was silent, but music emanated from where she was sitting.

"What are you listening to?" I asked, pointing to my ears.

"'Breathe,'" she said.

She removed the sound piece and walked over slowly, placing it against my ear.

> *I can feel the magic floating in the air.*
> *Being with you gets me that way.*
> *I watch the sunlight dance across your face.*
> *And I've never been this swept away.*

I pulled back. "A love song?"

She shrugged.

"You don't seem the love song type, if I might say that."

"I was in love just once, and this song reminds me of him. The artist is Faith Hill."

"Where is he today?" I asked.

"I'm not sure, Jonathan. He was from the country. Loved country songs. We met on a subway in New York City when he flew there on business, and he wore cowboy boots with his suit. That really stood out. He had been there only once in his entire life, so it was a chance encounter."

I smiled and shook my head. A woman hardened by the years. A New Yorker, no less, listening to Faith Hill.

Her eyes clouded over.

"So you didn't marry him."

"I wanted to, but he was already married. I never told him exactly how I felt because I just assumed it was an impossible situation. But it was electric. Not just lust, but *love*. True love." She closed her eyes.

"How do you know?" I asked.

"You know when you know, Jonathan. I know because I never felt that way again in my life, about anyone else. I had relationships, but I never felt that way."

"So you don't know where he is today? Maybe he'd want to know you're dying and that you loved him."

She shook her head.

"I came to the conclusion, years ago, that sometimes you meet someone who changes your life, but that doesn't mean that your life has to change."

I pondered that thought for a moment.

"But what if he wanted to say goodbye one last time?"

"To what end?" she asked, genuine curiosity in her voice.

"Because you could tell him how you really feel. How you've felt all these years. What if he feels the same?"

"What if?" she echoed, looking into closed hands. She seemed to be studying them, as if the crevices would provide answers. "If I told him, and he loved me back, what then? He'd be engulfed in grief. If he *had* loved me, at least all these years he's had the hope that I'd return. Hope is everything, Jonathan. You know that."

"You don't make much sense to me. You're not what you seem," I said.

"Are any of us?"

I stood, walked to my backpack, and reached inside. I pulled out the last protein bar and tore into it, famished.

※

"Are you angry?" I asked. "I mean, angry that your years will be cut short?"

"Oh, no," she said quickly. "Let's face it, I'd only have twenty more at the most, anyway. I'm 70 now. See, life is worth living, Jonathan. We're not guaranteed anything, you know, yet we come into this world feeling entitled as if we are. We arrive acting as if we've been handed a manual for life with a certificate that guarantees us a hundred years."

"But there are reasonable expectations . . . " I answered.

"Like what?"

"It's reasonable to think you'll live to the average lifespan for the country you live in. Don't we all expect we'll do better than that?"

"We do." She shook her head slowly. "Because we're selfish. Human beings are self-absorbed. We think we're in complete control of the beginning, the end, and everything in between. But we're not." She looked at me intensely. "Of course, you know that, too."

I thought of Boo and what Lacy and I had done with her the day before the accident. It was July, a month I would now detest for eternity.

We'd been standing in the park, feeding the ducks one day, and the next, they were gone. One day you're at the apex of your life, standing in all your glory before the sunrise, full of hope and possibility. The next you're at the sunset, darkness encroaching.

Night falls fast.

"Yes," she said. "It does."

I looked at her, knowing with complete certainty that I had not said a word.

※

"There's a helicopter coming to pick me up in an hour," she said finally. "My son rented one to allow me to fulfill this dream. He'll be taking me on home, if you'd like to hitch a ride."

"A helicopter?"

"Might as well travel in style, if it's one of your last

trips!" she replied with a grin.

"I guess you're right," I admitted. "Where're we headed?"

"New York. I live upstate, so we'll land at a small airport in the Adirondacks, and you can continue your journey from there. Or you're welcome to come stay with us."

I thought about her offer. I'd never been to the Adirondacks before and had always wanted to see them. But I had been gone for less than a week, and I wasn't ready to spend time around people I hardly knew.

"I'll take you up on the offer of a lift," I said. "But I want to go hike up into the mountains."

Marilyn smiled. "Whatever suits you!"

＊

An hour later the chopper landed about five hundred feet away. It was shiny and black, with stripes across the side and a compact cabin that appeared to seat no more than four. The blades cut through the desert sky, kicking up dust until they sputtered to a stop.

Marilyn tossed her backpack onto her shoulder and headed toward the helicopter. I followed.

She ducked into the cabin and sat in the back as if she'd done it before. The pilot motioned me into the seat beside him and handed me a headset to protect my ears. Marilyn buckled in, placed a wrinkled hand on the pilot's shoulder, and squeezed hard. He placed a gloved hand on hers and squeezed back.

"I'm Conrad," he said, smiling. "Ready to go?"

Before I could respond, the blades roared, much louder than I'd expected. As we lifted off, I felt a jolt of adrenaline rush through me, my body suspended. I felt alive, like I was being prodded out of a coma.

We soared over canyons and majestic white mountains. We dove deep through the center of long stretches of brown desert and watched a herd of animals below. We were headed east, although I didn't really care where we were headed because I had no expectations for the journey.

An hour into the flight, Conrad explained that we'd be landing at a remote airport to switch to a small Cessna he owned for the remainder of the journey. Once we arrived in New York, I would leave them and go my own way, I told him.

Floating over the clouds, I realized that at times I could still feel her, and I wondered if there was any difference in the scope of eternity between what was and what is, or what will be. Boo had only been on this earth for four short years, but her soul had been ancient, as if I'd known her for not one lifetime, but many.

Lacy and I had been connected from the start, not like it was with the other women I'd met and conquered, but *different*, as if our souls were intertwined.

A cord of three strands is not easily broken.

As the helicopter floated toward the horizon, I remembered what the shrink back in Orange County had said. Some people come into your life out of circumstance, while others arrive because they had to. They are there for your soul. They were sent to you. They were sent to deliver a message. To bring or to take away.

I glanced over at Conrad, effortlessly navigating the chopper through the clouds. He was the kind of man I'd wanted to be, the kind every man wanted to be—a James Bond type both men and women would be drawn to. He instantly reminded me of an old friend of mine from college. His name was Jason, and he had the same square jaw and rugged exterior. He had entered one relationship and then the next, with whatever woman he'd met at the time.

The last time I'd seen him he'd been through his second divorce and was on to another relationship.

Because of his good looks, women entered and exited based on geography or convenience, but never from selection.

I had told him my theory that convenience was the enemy of happiness. It led to settling, instead of sustaining. Jason had said that women were like gumballs and came in many colors. You find one and then another in the glass jar. You put in a quarter, own one, and then after a while you get tired of chewing, and it's inevitable that you'll move on to another.

"You have to listen to your heart," I told him, "instead of selecting someone who's convenient and happens to be in the right place at the right time. You have to choose someone you'd still want to be with if you had to travel to Dubai to see her. Only then will your heart be authentic.

"It's like the difference between choosing the milk in the front of the display case with the expired date on it, just because you need milk, rather than driving to a different store for the organic milk you really want."

Lacy was never easy. But she'd been worth it. We were light drawn to darkness, dark to light, like opposite sides of the same coin. Her moods varied because of her past. It had been a tragic childhood, and, as an adult, the memories remained. Sometimes she was day, sometimes night.

Day and night is still the same 24 hours.

✳

The chopper hovered over a tiny airport in a desolate brown field.

Music drifted in through the headset. It was an old song by Rush.

> *Thirty years ago, how the words would flow*
> *With passion and precision,*
> *But now his mind is dark and dulled*
> *By sickness and indecision.*
>
> *Some are born to move the world—*
> *To live their fantasies*
> *But most of us just dream about*
> *The things we'd like to be.*

C.S. Lewis once wrote that grief is a long valley, and that sometimes you wonder if the valley is a circular trench.

Conrad landed the helicopter gently, and we unloaded and waited inside a hangar while the Cessna was fueled for the remainder of our journey. When we boarded the small airplane, Marilyn was so alive—with eyes wide open—that it was impossible to think she was dying.

Her son navigated the small craft down the runway, and it lifted into the sky. Gliding in a completely different sensation from the ride before, my blood moved horizontally this time. He flew across different terrain and we coasted in silence.

Finally, I spied an airport in the center of a mountain range that was overflowing with green and thousands of trees. We dropped lower and touched down on a small runway.

Conrad removed his helmet and turned to me. His eyes were blue.

"Welcome to New York!" he said.

Chapter 3

THE STORM

Here briefly, in this forest shall you dwell . . .

—THE PURGATORIO

I woke from a dream at three in the afternoon and sat up for a while, staring out the window. A storm was coming, and as I watched the bending of the trees, I wondered if one of them would break.

✳

We'd landed in the heart of the Adirondacks, and when I asked an airport employee to recommend a hotel, he said he knew just the one. It was remote and at the edge of the lake.

It was a bit of trouble to get there, he said, but without snow it would be okay. His uncle owned it, the key would be under the mat, and the caretaker would be up to bring wood for the stove in the morning.

Marilyn and Conrad and I had embraced in a triple hug like old friends, standing in the small Adirondacks airport. People drifted by slowly, like souls floating past, unlike the way they scurried quickly to claim baggage in other airports. And it was in that moment that time stood still. I would not see them again, I realized. There was no past, no future. Only now.

One of us broke, and we wept like infants, as if a strong dam had set free.

The last words she said to me were catalogued in my brain, right below the last words Boo had said, and then Lacy. I was keeping a list now, an electronic Rolodex of last words.

I love you daddy.

How's our baby girl?

And then standing there in the airport . . .

"Some people who have decades to live are already dead inside, Jonathan. Right now I feel more alive than ever. Be alive, Jonathan, not one of the walking dead. Lessons of this sort cannot be taught; they come from one's own struggle to find truth."

✳

The taxi ride from the airport had taken us ten miles to the nearest cabin. The road wound deep into the forest through a row of tall maples, ending at a small gravel drive.

The cabin was more than I'd expected. A stone walk led up to the door, and a small garden with brightly colored flowers surrounded it. There were white pines everywhere, and it was wrapped in complete silence.

It had a traditional log exterior, and someone had painted the door candy apple red. Above the door was a handcrafted wood plaque with an inscription.

Lasciate ogne speranza, voi ch' intrate.

I pulled the key from under a brown welcome mat that had a smiling beaver on it, slid the key into the lock, and entered, stepping into a small open space that resembled a Thomas Kinkade painting I'd once purchased for Lacy, called "The End of a Perfect Day," with a woodstove, tin roof, and through the back window, a canoe visible in the back near the edge of a pond.

I felt a peace I hadn't felt in the desert.

※

Now I walked across the hard wood floor, my bare feet feeling the rawness.

How's our baby girl?

I felt a sense that I'd been there before, but I chalked it up to the comfort I'd always felt when I had visited my grandfather's cabin on the lake, decades earlier.

I love you daddy.

Some things remain in your DNA forever. I opened the door and walked outside again, stepping onto the small wood porch. I observed the way some of the trees swayed deeply, while others stood rigid. Like humans, each one moved slightly differently, changing with the shift of the wind.

Be alive, Jonathan.

I sat in the rocking chair and imagined those who had done the same thing a hundred years before, imagining the lives and messages we receive like one eternal thread, all connected. I thought of my brother, who had loved hunting and fishing in the mountains with our grandfather when we were young, while I had been content to skip rocks in the stream, unable to stomach the thought of killing a deer.

I considered calling him, but there was no telephone, and even if there were, what would I say? Everything was different now.

He'd be unable to understand my desire to escape.

He'd want to talk me into coming home, talk me back off the ledge of this new journey and into the normalcy of my abnormal existence.

But what would I go back to now?

I fell asleep again in the chair, sometime after four in the afternoon, and when I awoke, it was dark and the wind howled through trees. I had much to do, but couldn't. Much to say, but couldn't. Much to feel, but couldn't. The shrink back in California had said I'd entered a "dorsal vagal shutdown," which in plain civilian terms meant that I was frozen. The answer, she'd said, was social engagement via the ventral vagus nerve, accomplished by laughing or connecting with others.

Everyone, it seemed, had an answer.

My Christian friend Bob told me that isolation was the tool of the devil. That, although it seems like a gift, it's also a curse when we become too inwardly focused, withdrawn from life, disconnected. He'd said that the enemy can get to your emotions only after you've been isolated, a strategy used by the greatest war generals of all time. Isolate, then defeat.

✳

"How long you staying?"

The voice startled me, and I turned.

The man walked with a limp, one leg looking to be shorter than the other, and he was wearing a flannel shirt and high rubber boots over jeans. He shifted his weight to his good leg as he ambled up the path toward the cabin, stopping once to catch his breath.

"I been waitin' for you," he said, approaching the deck. He carried a long shovel, the end covered in mud.

"Really? But I . . . " I was about to say that I'd just arrived, that he couldn't have possibly known I'd be there because I hadn't known it myself. But my energy ran out. I had no more to give, no more explanations. He was a caretaker, it seemed. He'd leave the wood, shovel something, and be gone soon.

"I've got wood in the truck," he said, "to load up the stove."

"Go for it," I answered.

The man pulled the chair from the other side of the deck and dragged it over, slowly and painfully. I considered giving him a hand, but despite the apparent discomfort, he seemed to be doing fine. I guessed that he'd been there for years, probably the employee of some charitable and wealthy land baron who owned this cabin and the magnificent property surrounding it. The land, at least, would be worth about four million, I estimated.

"My name's Peter," he said, taking a seat and extending his hand. "After Saint Peter. Or Peter the Great. You choose." He laughed then. "You here for long?" He had a slight accent that I couldn't place.

"I don't know, Peter."

"What do you mean you don't know?"

"I may stay a month. I may stay a year."

"It'll be about five days, I suppose," he said, checking his watch.

I glanced at him curiously.

"You have someone else checking in in five days?"

"Nope."

With that, he stood slowly and entered the cabin. Through the open door I watched him walk into the kitchen and open a cabinet. There were a few cans of food there, and a flashlight. He reached for something and started back out.

"I keep some Jack in the cupboard," he said. "Want some?"

I shook my head. I hadn't drank since '91, when I almost wrapped my car around a tree after a birthday party for a friend. I hadn't been an alcoholic, but it was the moment that woke me up to the fact that I was seconds away from it. Being something and *not* being that thing, I had discovered, can be separated by a very fine line.

Peter poured me a shot of Jack Daniel's anyway from the large vintage bottle and poured himself one, too. He handed me a shot glass, and I took it, downing the harsh dry liquid all in one sip.

"Jack Daniel's is a legendary company," he said, settling into the other chair again. "The founder saved a small town with the distillery. The first bottle he produced cost less than two dollars."

"You a fan of trivia?" I asked.

"I'm a lifelong learner," he said, "and I like to know all I can." He poured me another shot and I drank it fast, feeling the burn down the back of my throat.

"So is that all you do? Sit up here and drink Jack Daniel's in the forest?"

He glanced over as if he were pondering his response.

"Sometimes it's a nice end to a perfect day," he said.

I looked at him and wondered. Something about this journey was becoming surreal. In the beginning, I hadn't known where I was going. I'd bought a ticket to somewhere I'd never been, walked for miles, and ended up in the desert with a woman who had less than a month to live. Now, here I was in a cabin at the opposite end of the country with someone entirely different.

Where would I be tomorrow?

The whole of it was hard to ignore.

"You need something for that wound on your face?" he asked.

I shook my head and instinctively touched it with my hand.

"Nah," I said. "You take care of this place?" I asked.

Peter nodded. He leaned back and with some effort hoisted his rubber boots high onto the porch railing.

"Do you know how I officially check in?" I asked. "I know they left the key under the mat, but I assume they'll want a credit card at some point."

"We'll get one from you on the day you leave," he said. "It's pretty laid back around here."

"Sounds good," I said. "Where you from?"

"Italy, originally. My parents were Italian immigrants, but I grew up in an orphanage upstate. I like it out here in the wilderness. It's lonely at times, but quiet, that's for sure."

"Are you married?"

He shook his head. "Oh no, not for me."

"Is it hard work up here in the winters, with the snow and all?" I asked. "Do the owners have a lot of vacationers coming in and out?"

"I'm the owner," he said.

I looked at him and laughed.

"Yeah . . . right."

Peter shrugged and poured another shot glass of Jack. Then he looked at me curiously.

"Why is that so hard to believe?"

I held out my glass, and he poured me another. I drank it down, then did it again.

"You really the owner?" I asked.

Peter nodded.

"You're good at prejudging people, aren't you," he said.

"I just asked if you were the owner," I countered.

"Yes, but you must find it impossible to believe that someone who looks as nondescript as me could have an MBA and own a multi-million dollar piece of property in one of the most expensive parts of New York."

"You have an MBA?"

"Sure do," he said. "It was an accident, really. Bad time in my life, when I didn't know what I wanted to be. I went back to school to try to find myself."

"And did you?"

"I did. But the MBA had nothing to do with it. That was all a big waste of time, if you ask me. I found this land in the mountains, and I knew I wanted to build on it. I built five cabins, then ten. Now I've got seventeen across a span of two hundred acres. It's worth millions."

"Wow." I thought of the risk and the guts and the determination it had taken to do all of that.

"There were a series of chance meetings that led me to this, of course. Before, I only *dreamed* about the mountains. But then I met people who inspired me along the way.

He looked directly at me.

"Son, there are people sent to all of us. Angels, you know. We all got 'em."

"You think?" I wondered if he heard doubt in my voice.

He nodded. "Guardian angels."

I laughed. "You really believe that?" I shook my head. "I don't believe in all that metaphysical stuff."

"So what you're really saying is that you don't believe in the things you can't see."

I shrugged. I wasn't sure anymore. To be certain, there were things that were unexplained. Things had happened that defied any sort of reason.

✳

In the days prior to the accident I'd been warned. I'd felt anxious, as if there was an unsettling in my soul.

Take a day off and spend it with Boo, I wrote into the memo section of my Blackberry. *These moments are all you have.*

Boo was asleep in the next room when I'd done that, and before I knew it, the day was gone again, and I had missed the chance. I never did take a day off.

In all of her four years of life, not one day.

Now, we were together but not.

"Peter, you're not what you seem," I observed.

"Jonathan, welcome to the Adirondacks. Stay awhile. You're going to leave better than you came."

Chapter 4

THE INTERSECTION

In an instant they were gone.

Team Taylor, up in flames just like that.

After the call I raced to the intersection and watched from the side of the road. Paramedics surrounded the car, and I dove into it through the window in a frantic search for Boo, flames tearing at my pant leg, the fire biting at the fabric of my shirt, searing it until it crumbled like ash.

Lacy was already gone. The ambulance had taken her away.

Someone, a paramedic maybe, pulled, pushed— maybe both—to get me out of the window of the Ford

Explorer. My upper body slid through the space where the other window had been on the opposite side as they dragged me by the arms over shards of glass and more flames.

My bloody face hit the pavement, and a chunk of glass lodged in the side of my cheek. The smoke stung my eyes, a shield of gray and black.

I turned back and saw the soccer ball sticker on the windshield, melting away.

A backpack on the ground?

A man stumbling?

Both cars were black, a mixture of metal bonded together as one.

When it was all over, I woke up in a hospital room, panicked and physically restrained. My face and arms were bloody, and I realized instantly that I'd have to play the game to get out.

"How are you feeling, Mr. Taylor?"

A handful of doctors hovered by the bed. A nurse held my hand, but her expression of compassion mixed with pity gave it all away.

They were gone.

"I'm numb," I said, and choked back a scream. "But I'm okay." The last part wasn't true.

A week later, the police report came in and there had been a witness—a fifty-year-old woman who said she'd never get over what she saw that day. A black F-150 had T-boned the Explorer after Lacy had forgotten to stop.

Forgotten? I read the lines on the photocopied report and knew it couldn't be right.

Forgotten? The witness reported that even after the impact, with the car upside down, the driver had reached into the backseat, fumbled and fought for her daughter's seat belt. Lacy had tried to save Boo, even while the paramedics were trying to save Lacy.

I continued reading.

> *The driver locked the car door when paramedics approached to try to remove her from the Ford Explorer. As flames engulfed the vehicle, she fought to unbuckle her daughter from the car seat.*

Warrior mom would not leave her baby girl.

Team Taylor, gone in an instant.

※

On day two at the cabin I found the ground coffee in the cupboard, along with a container of powdered cream and even the vanilla flavoring that Lacy liked. I figured out the coffee maker, and before long I was standing out on the front porch in my bare feet, watching the sun rise.

The grass was wet, and three squirrels fought or played in the pine trees in the yard. One ran fast, bouncing and swaying like an acrobat along the branches, with the others in hot pursuit. Across the sky, sailing one tree to another, then down the bark to the ground in a near-miss collision at the bottom.

I stood there in my boxers and t-shirt and felt the warmth of the coffee mug inside my palm. The forest was alive, bustling with gentle sounds. A crew of bullfrogs sang and gulped to each other from around the back of the cabin near the pond. Birds called loudly from every crevice and corner. I turned to step back inside but stopped there, frozen on the deck. I stared at the inscription above the door.

Lasciate ogne speranza, voi ch' intrate.

Latin? Italian? What did it mean?

If I'd been home, I'd have Googled it to figure it out in moments.

Here, I just pondered it awhile, then walked inside, pulled on the one pair of trousers I'd packed for the journey, and slid into my dirty t-shirt. I laced up my hiking boots over warm socks and set out around the back of the cabin toward the water. The ground was wet and slippery, and the canoe sat upside down at the edge of the pond near a small shed.

I wandered over, and, when I ducked inside, I saw two other canoes tied to ropes on a shanty dock. I stepped out onto the wood planks suspended above the water and walked down the dock, leaning forward to untie the boat closest to me. Inside it were two orange life jackets, paddles, and an empty Coke can. I worked the knot for a while until it unfastened and then slid the canoe closer and stepped inside. The craft rocked left and then right as I steadied myself and found my footing.

I sat down, hoisted the paddles into the water, and began rowing. My arms engaged in one full movement, then another, until I fell into a rhythm. A fluid movement, *one, two, three,* I counted silently, with each perfect circle. My shoulders felt strong, and I inhaled the fresh mountain air.

Get your body moving. Engage your senses.

Be alive, Jonathan.

I rowed for five minutes and then lifted the paddles out of the water and let the canoe glide . . . sliding like

an ice dancer across glass. I rowed more until I reached
the center of the pond and then sat in stillness and stared
above, into the sky, and then below into the water.

Nothingness. Just still.

No thoughts, no worries. Just water and sky.

I pulled off my t-shirt and dove into the pond, without thinking, and resurfaced feeling exhilarated! I didn't
care what was below. I stretched onto my back with my
body fully prone, my arms straight out above my head,
floating, and I stayed there for the longest time until the
canoe drifted out of reach, and then I dove down deep
into the pond and swam like a fish toward it, grabbing
onto the side. I pulled myself out and lay in the sun in
the center of the canoe, eyes closed.

After an hour or so I looked back to the shore to see
how far I'd gone. I saw a speck in the distance, but I had
drifted so far that I couldn't be sure what it was. It
looked like the shadow of a man, only it wasn't moving.
Was it a tree?

Suddenly the tree leaned slightly and moved in the
way I'd seen Peter amble along, and I knew it was him.
There he was, watching me.

I started rowing then, and my mind returned to the
police report. It was the last discovery after two pages of

eyewitness accounts, the one thing that I couldn't forgive. It was the last thing the police sergeant of twenty-one years had noted on that accident report that would remain fixed in my core forever.

Forgiveness would be impossible.

> *"Phone records from the driver report an outgoing text message from the cell phone of Mrs. Lacy Taylor at the time of impact, 12:01 pm."*

Forgiveness would be impossible.

※

I rowed the canoe around the lake for two more hours and thought of nothing, feeling as hollow as before despite the beauty. In the past months I'd had seconds—not minutes or hours, but seconds—of normalcy. But inevitably I'd remember what was real again, and the despair would settle back in. Nothing would be the same anymore.

I'd awaken in the morning from a full and rare night of sleep, only to realize upon waking that I was all alone in this new life.

Sometimes, five seconds can change your life forever.

※

I continued to row through thick reeds along the shore on the far side of the pond and then out of them into the very heart of the pond again. I lay back down in the canoe and felt the heat of the October sun on my face. The morning had been chilly, but by midday it was as warm as a summer afternoon.

Finally, I rowed back in an even gait toward the boathouse on the other side. When I arrived, Peter was waiting for me, shaking his head like my grandfather used to do, decades before.

"You look like a drowned rat," he said. "Are you crazy? Jumping into that pond with your boots on? Gonna take days now to dry them out." He limped over and tied a slipknot in the rope and secured the canoe against the dock alongside some buoys.

"Need anything?" he asked, still shaking his head in disbelief.

I smiled. "Nope, I'm doing great Peter, thanks."

Just some solitude, I thought. *A day without you checking in on me.*

"Not Peter," he said. "Call me Pete." He turned to move away, set his good foot in the dirt and pivoted slightly on that leg, moving the other leg with the help of his hand. He started up the hill, back to his old truck. I watched him amble slowly until he reached it and opened the door.

"Wait!" I shouted, running toward him. "I have a question for you." By the time I reached the old pickup I was out of breath.

"What's the inscription above the door?" I asked. "The cabin door." It was the only thing I really wanted to know at that moment.

Pete looked down at the ground. "Oh, you noticed that, did you?"

I nodded.

"That's Dante," he said. "The great Italian poet."

"What does it mean?"

He stepped back and steadied himself on the truck door for support, and it groaned at the rusty hinges. He drew in a deep breath.

"It means 'Abandon all hope, ye who enter here,'" he said slowly.

I just looked at him.

"Perfect," I said sarcastically. "Figures."

"What?"

"Well, what the hell kind of message is that for a cabin?"

"Oh, don't look so forlorn," Pete said. "It's not like you've checked into the Bates motel or something like that."

"Even so, what kind of inscription is that for a cabin in the woods? Do you have messages of doom above the doors of all of your cabins, just to welcome your guests?"

Pete chuckled, and rubbed his leg a bit, stretching it out.

"Oh, you're a hoot," he said wryly. "Nope. Just this one."

"Why?"

"You sure have a lot of questions," he observed.

"It just seems like a strange inscription to stick above the door of a vacation spot."

"Well, I suppose it does," he admitted. "That's a famous quote, Jonathan. Dante wrote in a form called *terza rima*, where three sets of lines are done in an interlocking rhyme format. He was exiled by the Italian government, and it was during that time of isolation that he wrote *The Divine Comedy*, about a man's loss of direction in his life. In the book, the traveler encounters the spirit of a poet in the forest. That spirit, named Virgil, guides him to the gates of hell, and that's where the inscription appears."

"I still don't get it."

"Don't get what?" he asked.

"I don't get why you decided to put that line above your cabin door. It seems contrary to the whole vibe of this place."

"We don't always need to 'get' things, Jonathan. Sometimes there's mystery in life, and we just have to embrace the not knowing."

"But your guests . . . "

Pete interrupted.

"Son, my leg is getting tired. I can only stand on it for a short while. Mind if I sit?" He slid backward through the open door and onto a torn leather seat, then continued. "You see, the guests who come here are at some intersection in their lives. Not sure what it is about this particular cabin, but it's true. Those who end up here have had a defining moment. They're in search of something. In that process, during the journey, it's inevitable that they'll have to go through hell to come out on the other side. Most of the time they have to transcend painful memories of some sort or event they've been through, to be whole again, to put all of the fragments of their soul back together.

"That's the reason for the sign. One must abandon hope, if necessary, and let go of everything they once knew. Sometimes it takes a season of brokenness in order to find the joy and beauty that comes after transformation. To go from where you are to where you need to be. The sign signifies that process.

"People come here to escape or to find themselves," he finished, "just like you did."

"How do you know so much about me?"

"I just know."

"But I didn't tell you that." I couldn't decide whether to be angry, or just creeped out.

"There's more in the universe than just words, Jonathan. There are things we can't see. For ages, philosophers and scientists alike have studied the brain, the soul, body language, and the subconscious energy we emit. Words aren't everything.

"In fact, sometimes words aren't necessary at all."

Chapter 5

PETE'S CABIN

*"Whatever is has already been and
what will be has been before . . . "*
— ECCLESIASTES

On day three at the cabin I stayed in bed until the sun forced itself in through the windows. The sheets were silky and the down comforter smelled fresh and lay heavy on my chest, enveloping me. There were four pillows, and I used them all. It was hard to leave the bed, but finally I climbed out and slid across the hard wood floor to the kitchen to make coffee, and then I crawled back to the bed again.

I was instantly asleep. I dreamt of the accident scene then, as real and up close as if I were standing there. But in this version, a man walked up to me on the side of the road. He spoke.

"Tomorrow is a word on the fool's calendar, Jonathan."

I woke up hours later remembering the dream clearly. The coffee maker was off and the coffee cold. I thought about the words the man had said in the dream and tried to figure out their significance.

Still mulling it over, I walked outside to the front deck and was startled by the majestic beauty that surrounded me. Everywhere, there were trees of gold. I had heard that the forests of the Adirondacks were more vast than Yellowstone, the Grand Canyon, and Yosemite combined. Bears and moose were said to be abundant, and the original settlers who came into this wild frontier built their cabins by hand, using tree trunks, branches, and stones they found in the woods.

Breathing deeply, I exhaled and stared deep into the trees, and then turned, transfixed by the inscription above the door.

Abandon all hope, ye who enter here.

Six months ago I might have had hope. But looking

back, there were a lot of other things I had been lacking. I was forty-two then, with a thriving career but no real purpose. Some days I'd get up and go to work, then return after dark and never even see Lacy and Boo, since they would already be in bed. The people I worked with had become my friends, but only because I didn't have time for anyone else.

Working to make money had become my sole motivation in life, but I never questioned it.

Lasciate ogne speranza, voi ch' intrate.

Someone—and I could guess who—had left a basket of red apples on the welcome mat, and I plucked one out, bit into it, then took the entire basket inside and placed it on the counter. Falling back into bed, I finished the apple and tossed the core across the room into the trash can, sinking it in one throw.

I drifted off once more, and when I woke up again I wondered if I was edging into serious depression. I laughed, but at nothing in particular.

How many days would I linger in hopelessness?

✳

On the fourth day in the Adirondacks, I awoke to a loud banging at the door. Peeking out of the bedroom and through the living room, I could see Pete's shadow through a window, and he knocked again.

He bent over slowly, then straightened before turning away and clumping down the path.

I ambled back to the bed and waited for the sound of his old Chevy to descend the gravel drive and fade into the distance. I envisioned him shaking his head, wondering about this strange guest he had.

Dragging myself out of bed again, I went to the window and peeked out to find some fire logs and a basket on the front porch. Opening the door, I picked up the basket. In it were some Neosporin ointment and a note from Pete.

> *This is for that scar on your face. Use it, and*
> *it will heal up better.*

I squeezed some of the gel out of the tube onto my finger and slid it across my cheek. The cut was still partly open, and it burned.

I went back to bed.

※

Sometime in the night I woke to the pain rumbling through my insides. It was good to feel the pain of hunger, good to feel my muscles tighten, and I thought about all the people who survived in the wilderness without food and all of the people in the world who couldn't survive a day without a drive-through fast-food meal.

I thought about the men who'd been out here in the wilderness years before, eating off the land, making branch houses with their hands, dirt under their finger-nails, burying their dead in the back.

And then my thoughts drifted back to Boo and the funeral, and the food that streamed in and out of the house, turning the scent of the air into a mixture of mashed potatoes and meat and desserts so nauseating I hadn't cared if I ate again for years.

Before the Last Supper, Jesus had foreseen the events that led to his death. The Last Supper was symbolic of the way we'd remember it all forever.

A meal, a celebration, death.

✳

The next day while I sat on the front porch, I heard the familiar sound of an engine and the gravel kicking up, and before I could retreat, a large brown UPS truck pulled into sight. The driver pulled it close to the cabin, jumped out, and tossed me an envelope.

"Peter J. Spinelli?"

"Well . . . I . . . " Before I could protest, he shoved a pen toward me. "Sign here," he said, and I scrawled my name on the paper on the clipboard. He smiled, hopped back into the truck, and pulled away.

Moments later Pete pulled up in the Chevy, and I watched him take an eternity to swing his bad leg over the front seat onto the driveway and twist himself out of the truck. He waved cheerfully, moving slowly toward me.

"We got a delivery?" he asked. "Saw the truck in the distance."

I nodded, and handed over the package.

"Haven't had one of those in three years," he said.

"Really? You haven't had a delivery in three years?"

"Don't have much need for it," he said, tearing into the envelope. "Go into town for the mail and to pick up everything I need up here."

I sat down and watched him from the rocking chair. It creaked back and forth on the deck, its old legs like Pete's, slow but steady.

His face went colorless.

"Well?" I asked impatiently. He jerked, as if he'd forgotten that I was there. Then he looked at me.

"It says my biological mother has died. It's a notice from an executor of her estate."

"But . . . I . . . You said you grew up an orphan," I replied. "How did they find you?"

Pete shook his head, and his eyes welled with tears.

"I don't know," he said. "I don't know." Then he fell silent, just staring at the piece of paper, and I found it strangely unsettling. Usually I couldn't get him to stop talking.

"Where is the package from?" I asked, working to fill the space.

"Italy. It says that I need to be there in three days. I need to get on a flight and attend a court hearing in Rome." Then he looked up at me again, and there was a strange expression on his face. "You want to go?"

"Yeah, that's funny." I got up to go into the cabin.

"No, really—you want to go?"

I turned and looked at him. Tears spilled out of the corners of his eyes again.

"I don't think I can make it alone, what with my bad leg and all. But I *should* go. I should go to find out who she was."

I closed my eyes.

"Aw, Pete, I don't have the money to go on a trip like that. It's an impossible request."

"Impossible?"

"Impossible."

We sat silently for a long time.

"Think about what you just said," Pete replied. "Impossible. *Nothing* is impossible. Give me a break. I'm loaded. I've got *tons* of money. And you've got tons of time. You can go with me, help me make the trip, help me with the bags, and then go on your own way."

He stood up, and went inside the cabin. He came back with the bottle of Jack.

"Maybe this will help convince you?"

I shook my head and lifted my feet up over the wood balcony railing.

"It's not going to happen Pete. I don't need to go to Italy. I don't need to go anywhere."

He poured me a shot glass of the brown liquid, and we drank one down, then another. It felt good.

The temperature dropped considerably, and Pete suggested we move inside and build a fire. I grabbed the logs he'd left by the door a day earlier and tossed them into the stone fireplace in the living room.

"You got a match?" I felt the heat of the Jack spreading through my arms, warming my fingers.

Pete set his glass down on the wood end table, removed his thick flannel overshirt and ambled toward the hearth unevenly, shaking his head.

"No, that ain't right," he said. "Weren't you ever a boy scout?"

"Just give me a match, Pete. It'll light."

"But that's not how you build a proper fire," he insisted.

I settled down into the leather chair by the fireplace and lifted my boots onto the ottoman.

"OK, Houdini, show me your magic," I said, motioning toward the pile of logs. "It's all wood. Just add a flame and it'll spark, I would think."

"Nope." Pete worked to arrange the logs in a triangular fashion, pulling mine out and re-positioning them again in his own way, like a small version of a teepee. He started with one log in the center and stacked the others carefully at an angle beside it.

"See, it all starts with the foundation," he said. "Just like our lives. If you don't put the logs onto the stack correctly in the first place, it's too late once you've lit the match." He carefully positioned the last log, found a box of matches in the kitchen, and rolled up some paper, lighting it.

"The outer logs can burn for hours independently, and if they're not touching the center log, you've got no bonfire. You've just got random logs that don't connect with the other ones. You need to build it right to get the full effect."

I watched Pete's fire spark, then ignite. Before long it burned passionately in deep red tones that sent smoke swirling upward through the stone chimney. The scent of pine filtered into the cabin, enveloping us.

Pete settled onto the couch and motioned toward his creation.

"Now *that*, my friend, is one of life's hidden treasures—the simplicity of knowing how to build a fire and passing it on. Next time you build a fire you'll do it that way, I bet."

I smiled, and I was sure he was right.

"And you'll think of me," he added.

I stared into the blaze, hypnotized by the flickering of the flame.

"My brother can make a fire like that," I said, thinking out loud. "He was always the meticulous one.

Earned a badge in boy scouts for building a fire when we were kids."

"So you have a brother?"

I nodded, and tears began to gather at the corners of my eyes. Pete noticed and pulled his cell phone out of the pocket of his shirt.

"You want to ring him up? Brag about where you are?" He smiled, no doubt trying to make me feel lighter.

"No," I said. He looked at me curiously. "It's a long story."

Pete shrugged, placed a hand on his jaw, and scratched down the side.

"So are you sad?" I asked, changing the subject.

"I don't know," he responded. A line of stubble had started across his chin and he tugged at it for a while. He looked up as if he was pondering my question, or searching for answers. I thought then that he was the most open person I'd ever met. He had no desire to impress anyone, as if the years on the mountain had erased his ego.

"I don't know if I'm sad or happy, Jonathan. Happy to be found, finally. Happy that I was recognized by my mother in some small way. You have no idea what it's like to not know where you come from and to have no connection to anyone.

"The orphanage records were destroyed in a fire years ago, and all of my family history was erased. So I have no idea how they found me. Still, I'm happy that I'll finally learn more about that connection.

"But I suppose I'm a bit sad at the same time." He pointed out the window to the trees in the front yard, where two bluebirds were engaged in a battle. "Look at that!" he said excitedly. He rose from the couch and walked outside, and I followed.

The first bird swooped low, straight toward the other, then flew away with the second bluebird fluttering in pursuit. They jaunted up toward a branch, then under it gracefully, jabbing back and forth at each other.

"We've all got a war within us," Pete said. "Like two warring bluebirds."

"You're like a wise old monk," I said, smiling. "You know that? You always have a way with words. Two bluebirds, eh?"

Pete nodded.

"That's right. And sometimes we let the bluebirds fight and rip us to shreds inside, when we should stop it from happening."

I rolled my eyes.

"Why do I feel a lesson coming on?"

"It's *all* a lesson, Jonathan." He stood up and lifted his hands to the sky. "Look around!" he said excitedly, with more passion than I'd seen from him before. "We're *alive*! Look at this majestic beauty we woke up to this morning." He turned to me. "How many summers or falls do you have left Jonathan? Maybe twenty? Thirty? There's no time for warring emotions. We need to make a decision to be happy, despite the death of our dreams. We need to be willing to create new ones."

I sat down and leaned far back in the rocker, pushing with my legs until the forks were lifted off of the deck. I inhaled and stayed there for a while, eyes closed. Quite frankly, I didn't want to think about my dreams. I felt anger rising inside, against Pete, against God, against the world.

I pushed it down.

Pete spoke again.

"I'll get over my sadness today," he said, "get on my plane tomorrow, and let it go. We humans place too much value on our emotions, and we let them rule our lives and wreak havoc in them."

"Sometimes life wreaks havoc on your emotions whether you let it or not," I shot back.

"Yes, our circumstances can be tragic. But your emotion isn't who you are. Often we humans make the mistake that it is." He stared into the trees, where the sun had dropped, casting an orange glow through the branches. He looked back at me, and his brown eyes were wide and young, the eyes of a twenty year old. What I felt at that moment was indescribable.

"We believe that emotion is who we are, but it's not that way at all," he continued. "That's a trap. You can get trapped in your emotions until they become your identity, until you've lost all direction and your compass is off kilter." He stood and walked to the wood railing, placing his hands on it. "You've been sad since you arrived. You have a heavy spirit of darkness all over you. How long are you going to let yourself live in that?

"Why do you think it's your right to ask?" I said angrily.

We sat in silence for a long time.

Then Pete turned and swept his hand across the sky.

"Can you imagine being persecuted for your beliefs in a world as beautiful as this?" he said, changing the subject.

"What?" I was starting to wonder if he'd had too much to drink. "Is this another one of your philosophical diatribes, because if it is, just give me another hit right now." I held the shot glass out toward him.

"In Greece, in 399 BC," he continued, ignoring the glass, "Socrates was prosecuted for his teachings. The government charged that he was corrupting the youths of Athens. At his trial, Socrates said that the unexamined life is not worth living. He was sentenced to death."

"Did you read about that in his book?"

"Oh, no, my friend. In fact, Socrates never even *wrote* a book of his own. Plato was there, and recorded it all."

"The unexamined life is not worth living," I echoed. "What does that mean, anyway?"

"Well, most people go through their lives on autopilot. They get up, go to work, go home, sleep, get up, go to work, always reacting instead of being intentional about their lives. Some of them let people in when they shouldn't, while others do the exact opposite, closing themselves off and hanging onto toxic people or feelings longer than they should. Either end of the spectrum is destructive.

"Our society is driven by a complete, apathetic lack of intentionality."

I looked around at the forest, marveling at the whole thing. Just a few days ago, in the desert. Now here, in the mountains with someone I'd never met before I arrived, drinking whiskey when I hadn't drank in years. Yet somehow it all seemed right. Stepping out, letting life lead.

"So most people don't examine their lives, is what you're saying," I asked.

"Exactly," he replied. "And some people examine them *too much*."

I hesitated.

"Is this your roundabout way of trying to get me to go to Italy to be your bag boy?" I asked. "I know that's what you're getting at."

"It might just be time for you to help a friend," he said with a grin. "Some people are so self-centered that they're always drowning in their own pain. They're so focused on themselves that they never contemplate giving to someone else. But that might be exactly what they need."

"I think I've been a mixture of both in my life." I said.

"Haven't we all." He looked somber again. "Your journey of self-discovery is worth it all, Jonathan, *despite* the pain. Come to Italy with me. It'll be just another adventure."

I looked at him and rolled my eyes.

"A plane ride with you?"

Pete threw his head back and laughed.

"What else have you got to do?"

I shook my head. He had me there. My muscles felt atrophied from lying in bed for more than two days. He was right.

What else have I got to do? If I was honest with myself, nothing.

Chapter 6

THE JOURNEY

*Sometimes you meet someone who
changes your life, but it doesn't mean
your life has to change.*

Every man has his journey.

Che Guevara embarked on a motorcycle journey through the Andes in the '50s, a controversial figure who crossed several countries. His life-changing journey began in Buenos Aires, and he traveled across borders into Chile and then across rugged mountains to Machu Picchu.

I once read a newspaper article about a man who backpacked halfway around the world after his business failed because he had nothing left. In the journey he found that he needed nothing materially and was able to survive on very little.

We journey because we can, and sometimes we journey because we have no other choice. Sometimes I thought of Lacy and saw that, sometimes, it's another human being who sets us off on a journey. Was I like Manolete, the great bullfighter, who just didn't know when to give up? Or would I journey to the end of the earth and find peace?

✳

At the departure gate in New York, Pete had handed me all of the travel documentation along with the boarding cards his travel agent had sent over. We'd be flying into the Otopeni airport in Bucharest, and I would help him get through security and the lengthy customs process, plus haul around the one small bag he had packed. I'd get him loaded onto a train that would take him to Rome because it had been a boyhood dream of his to take a train.

We'd part ways and I'd be free to follow my own path into the mountains of Transylvania, to stay in a hostel Pete had arranged for me. He would meet me three days later.

"Transylvania?" I had asked. "Why there?"

"Just seems like an interesting place," he said. "And since we'll be flying in and out of Bucharest, it makes sense."

✳

The flight attendant walked through the cabin. Her navy blue vest matched the rest of her outfit, which included a skirt, hose, and a jacket layered with necklaces. Before, I would have watched her with different eyes like the other men who traveled on business and pretended to be reading the sports section while they were fixated on the cleavage that was spilling out.

Now I saw everything differently. Her shoes were thick; the vest too tight on an aging body. The energy of the men who leered at her, hoping for attention or casual conversation, was disgusting. It was as if I were wearing new glasses.

Pete settled into the seat beside me, closest to the window, and fell asleep like a newborn the moment the engines hummed. His eyelids fluttered, and, as I watched him, I felt a softness I'd never felt for another man except my grandfather.

Before he dozed off, though, he looked over and whispered.

"I've got some advice for you son, and I'd like you to listen up. There's a reason you're sitting here with me, an old man you just met on a mountain."

"Yeah?" I asked. "What is it? It better be good."

"People come into and go out of your life. Some are worth keeping, and even fighting for, and others need to be let go. That's a very important lesson my friend. You need to find a way to understand who's there to add value to your life, and who was sent to take it away. If someone is taking away from you, let him go. It's his season to leave you. If some emotion is taking away from you, let it go, too."

I stared at my friend and pondered his words.

Let it go.

The most liberating thing about him was that we hadn't talked about my past, and that he hadn't actually required anything of me, which meant we made a good pair. I had nothing to give, and he had nothing to ask.

He fell asleep shortly thereafter, and I stared past him out across the tarmac as the jet engines roared and the pilot backed the aircraft out of the gate, proceeded down the runway, and lifted into the sky.

I felt a tingling in my soul, a sense of nervousness coupled with disbelief that I was really doing this.

Am I really flying halfway across the globe?

※

A couple of hours into the flight the attendant came over and asked if I needed anything.

"I'll have a Coke," I said.

"You bet," she replied. "We'll be serving dinner soon."

Pete stirred, turned his head, and then fell back into a deep sleep. I read the remnants of the *London Financial Times* that someone had left in the seat back pocket and settled in to watch a movie. The plane was loaded with passengers of various nationalities, and many of them fell asleep right away. Others read or listened to music that filtered through headphones, and the flight attendants served a three-course meal, including chocolates.

After several hours, Pete woke up and tapped me on the arm.

"Good flick?" he asked.

"It's okay," I shrugged and removed the headphones from my ears. "You have a nice nap? You missed dinner."

"I had a dream," he said.

"Anything good?"

He wiped his eyes. His hair was disheveled on one side and stuck to the top of his forehead.

"I dreamt that I was standing on a rainbow," he said. "It was like I was floating above the clouds."

"Your mind is a crazy place to be."

"Dreams have vital importance, you know. You should listen to them. Some are prophetic."

"I don't dream much anymore . . . " I lied, remembering the man who had spoken to me in a dream. "But I used to when I was a kid."

"That's because children are magical thinkers." His expression was serious. "When we were young we didn't have the stress to keep us awake at night."

"I suppose. So what would Freud say about your dream?"

He pondered it for a minute.

"Oh, I don't know," he shrugged. "Maybe there's a rainbow ahead. A new life, awaiting us on our journey."

I stared at my new acquaintance.

"I've never met anyone quite like you, Pete. You have a uniquely optimistic way of looking at things."

He grinned and turned and stared out the window. The plastic was marked with long scratches from the elements, the result of years of takeoffs and landings.

The pilot spoke loudly through the intercom three

decibels higher than it needed to be, as if someone had brushed up against the volume button by accident.

"We'll be landing in the capital city of Bucharest, Romania, in just under two hours."

"Have you ever been to Romania before?" I asked Pete.

He shook his head. "Nope."

"I imagine it's poor, but beautiful."

"The mountain region in Transylvania is supposed to be one of the most majestic in the world," he said. "The average salary there is about $50 to $100 a month, yet the country's literacy rate is upward of 95 percent. Higher than ours."

"And we think we're the richest country in the world."

He laughed. "Oh, far from it. Not materially, and not in natural assets."

"We do have wealth, though; you've got to admit that."

"We have the *appearance* of wealth. We have debt, is what we have. And other countries, like Israel and Romania, have rich natural resources that are unimaginable in our corner of the world." He looked excited as he spoke. "This is going to be a great trip, Jonathan. I sense something major is about to occur in our lives, and it's going to be one helluva ride."

I didn't reply.

※

The airplane hit the tarmac in Bucharest, and the fuselage shook. The pilot apologized for the rough landing, and soon we disembarked and stood in the line at customs. I carried Pete's bag as we passed through, and I helped him through the terminal and found a luggage cart that he could push to the curb.

We shook hands and I clutched the envelope with the address for the hosteria Pete had arranged for me in the small town of Brasov.

"Are you sure you can make it on your own?" I asked.

"No problem from here, son. I've got help waiting on the other side. How about you? Are you sure you can make it on your own?" he asked, smiling.

Nodding, I walked with him outside to where a hired car was waiting to take him to the Gara de Nord station in Bucharest. It would cost a bit more than 48 euros for the journey, and the attorney managing the estate in Italy had agreed to send a car to meet Pete on the other end, when he arrived at the train station in Rome.

I joked with him about the irony of his situation.

Here he was, inheriting money in a will, when he already had more money than most people could imagine.

Pete stood by the hired car, a newer model black Lincoln.

"Only the rich get richer," I said. "It's not fair."

"It's all about trade-offs," he replied.

"Such as?"

"I've been given financial prosperity, but not love. You were given a marriage and love, but maybe not other things. Some people are blessed with great intellect, others great physical or athletic ability."

I pondered what he had said, thought about what I'd been given in life, and what had been taken away. While I was doing so, Pete ducked into the car and waved at me through the window as it drove off.

With that I stood at the curb of the Otopeni airport terminal with my backpack, surrounded by the sights and sounds of a bustling day and a crowd of people speaking languages that were foreign to me. I was immediately approached by a small man who waved frantically toward his car, a silver box with a dented passenger door. The side window had been blown out and was covered with plastic that had been secured with electrical tape. He flung open the door and said something I didn't understand.

"American? American? We go."

I shrugged, slid into the car, and looked down at the paper Pete had given me.

"Brasov?" I said. The man nodded excitedly, got in, gunned the engine, and sped away.

"Da! Da! Brasov." He repeated the same thing several times and pulled out into traffic, negotiating a roundabout aggressively. He cut off several cars and pulled onto a rustic two-lane highway that was straight for miles, swerving once to miss a small horse-drawn cart loaded with cages of chickens.

My driver laid on the horn as we passed and shouted something to the farmer driving the cart. I braced myself in the back by gripping the door handle as he zipped into the next lane to pass the cars in front of us, one by one. My heart raced as I watched a large truck approach head on, barely missing us at the last moment. He did this several more times, swerving one way and then the other, often directly into the lane with oncoming vehicles. Each time he and the other driver pressed on their horns, shouting, speeding recklessly past.

We passed a large white factory and desolate open fields, and, ahead in the distance, I could view the dark shadows of a mountain region, which I knew to be the

Carpathians. Pete had described the history of the mountains and the lore of Transylvania, saying that now its castle was somewhat of a tourist destination, despite the scarcity in the region.

It was a complex country, with rugged terrain and deep rivers, and a thriving ski area where the Italians came to vacation. The town of Brasov itself was a medieval village with gothic churches, surrounded by mountains on all sides.

The driver turned off the main road and drove for a while down cobblestone streets, pulling over abruptly at a curb in front of some old buildings.

"Basilica Negro," he announced, pointing to a tall cathedral with remnants of bullet holes in the side. The structure was carved with ornate sculptures and a magnificent spire jutting into the sky.

"*Unde mergi?*"

I shook my head. I did not understand.

The man waved his hands in the air and motioned toward one building, and then down another street in a completely different direction.

"*Unde mergi?*"

I pointed to the address on the slip of paper. The man took it from my hand.

"Ah, yes, da! Da!" He put the car back into gear and sped around a corner up a narrow cobblestone street, parking in front of a white concrete townhouse. Then he jumped out and grabbed for my backpack.

"No, thanks," I said, hanging on.

"Da! Da! I carry you," he insisted, trying English.

Finally I let the shoulder strap slide down my arm, and he hoisted it over his back and scurried up a set of stairs. A small girl wearing a tattered dress played on the steps, and up and down the street women in long dresses passed by, their heads covered with scarves. Following the driver, I stopped at the top stair and waited as he banged on the door.

It flung open, and a small black boy ushered us into a parlor where he took the bag and motioned us to follow him down the hall. Long and lanky, with limbs like a praying mantis, he moved silently and led us to a small bedroom, placing my backpack on the wood floor just inside. When I turned around, he was gone.

The taxi driver remained in the doorway, and I fished several bills of the local currency, the ron, from my pocket and handed them over. The man bowed in thanks and left.

Chapter 7

THE GARDEN

I closed the door and surveyed the small space. The room was stark, but the bed linens offered a brilliant white coverlet with the whitest sheets beneath. There was a solitary armoire and a window that overlooked a court-yard below.

When I peered down, I saw the boy standing there, working in a garden. It was dirt, mainly, and he used a rough hand trowel to shift it back and forth, turning the soil. Every once in a while he kneeled down, and I watched as he used his hands to spread it evenly and then back again over small green plants. It was hard to tell what they were.

I decided to change clothes and venture out. I pulled on a pair of Levi's and a fresh shirt and headed down the stairwell into the main house, where a large woman waited. I smiled at her, but she didn't smile back. She was about sixty, with a traditional headscarf and a skirt that fell below her knees over clunky black shoes. She nodded slowly as I passed, then went back to sweeping the wood floor.

"Hello," I said, and she mumbled something I couldn't understand in response.

I stepped outside into the fresh air, and the boy approached from nowhere, his fingernails layered in mud.

"Mr. America!" he said, smiling.

"You know English!" I said, taken aback.

The old woman came out and stood at the top of the stairs. Her face was frozen in a scowl, and she yelled something at the boy, who replied back in what seemed to be Romanian.

"*Noapta Buna.* It's okay Mrs. B.," he said, going back and forth from English to Romanian for my benefit, which only seemed to anger her more. But before long the old woman disappeared back inside.

"What's she mad about?" I asked.

"She doesn't want me to come in with dirty hands," the boy said. "She always worries about things before they happen." I thought about that for a moment, then just nodded.

"What's your name?" I asked.

"Solomon," he said. "Like the king."

"The king?"

"Yes. Solomon was a great king, one of the greatest of all time." The boy wiped his hands on his pants, and the dirt came crumbling off.

"How old are you?" I asked.

"*Zece.*"

I looked at him curiously.

"Sorry," he said. "I am ten. How old are you, Mr. America?"

"You know where I can get a cup of coffee?" I asked, dodging the question. "Maybe a bakery or a café?"

The boy pointed.

"Down the street, Mr. America. We go together. I show you." He put down the garden tool and walked me down the street in silence. I breathed in the fresh air and followed him to a bakery where I ducked inside and managed to order a muffin and the blackest coffee I'd seen.

After that we walked down narrow cobblestone streets with our faces to the sun, the world around us easy and intimate. Solomon led me up streets lined with terraces, where the locals gathered outdoor at the cafés and in the square talking, and gesturing animatedly. The houses were tall and narrow, some decorated with bright flowers in window pots, and I imagined the way Marilyn would have photographed the place if she could have seen it.

"You like football?" he asked abruptly.

I looked at him.

"I'm not good at it, no. I like watching it on television I suppose . . . " It had been a long time since I'd seen any football, but my thoughts went back to the last game I had watched, with the Giants against the Cowboys.

"We go now," he said, suddenly excited. "We go! Follow me!"

I followed him down the street, and we walked for what seemed like a couple of miles until we turned into an open-air stadium that was jammed with people. A soccer match was in full play, and I handed some bills over to a ticket taker before I realized that Solomon had led me into a scheme by asking me to take him to a game.

But his attitude was so engaging that I couldn't bring myself to be angry.

"You thought it was football, Mr. America. In our country *futbol* is soccer."

The stadium was lively, filled with more people than I'd been with in a long time. Men lined the field, wearing camouflage army uniforms like the ones our soldiers wore in the States. Only these uniforms were all blue camouflage instead of green, a dark navy mixed with a lighter shade of sky blue. They had machine guns across their backs, and each one wore a thick black belt with a pistol secured to it.

At first their presence unsettled me, but I soon relaxed and found myself enjoying the game.

﹡

The next day Victorita—the old woman the boy called Mrs. B.—made an elaborate breakfast at the table of hard-boiled eggs, bread, and Coca-Cola.

I quickly learned that the Coca-Cola was considered the ultimate in luxury for an American guest, since the Romanians viewed it as a symbol of what we liked. In every household I visited in the days to follow, friends of Victorita and her husband Cornell would offer me Coca-Cola and hard-boiled eggs, or sometimes if it was a special occasion, meat with carrots. The meat was boiled in water like a stew over the stove, and the carrots were tender, mixed in.

Each night when I went to bed, the pipes sang loudly, the sounds of water cranking through them.

When I needed to wash my hair, I did so in the spigot that came out from the bottom of the tub because there was no shower, and I took hand baths with a small cloth I found in my room. The house shared one bathroom, so at times I would find it occupied and go back to my room and wait.

In the mornings, I took to the habit of waking up and observing Solomon from my window, which looked out into the courtyard where he worked in the garden.

I tried to figure the boy out because each day he was up hours earlier than anyone else, just to water the garden and till the soil. It seemed like a passion or a hobby for him, and he worked with a small broken hand plow to till the dirt, over and over again.

Victorita and Cornell, whom Solomon called Mr. A., earned extra money from guests like me who periodically found the hostel, and although I'd never once seen her smile, Victorita worked tirelessly to make sure every need of the household was taken care of.

Solomon came and went as he pleased and seemed to have no schedule for school. He'd said he worked in the streets earning money, and, as I watched him one day in the town square, I realized that his chosen profession was that of a beggar or more aptly, a con artist who approached tourists and worked them over with his gift of words. He convinced them to give him the money, which he brought back to his Romanian family.

Solomon told me that the couple had taken him in a few years earlier and put a roof over his head. He had been a street gypsy, and he'd agreed to work in exchange for a room. He said it had taken him three days to convince Victorita not to report him to an orphanage instead. First he had worked sweeping her halls and stairs in the mornings, then tilling the garden, and then he brought home money from his work on the street until he was too valuable for her to let him go.

He wore cloth shoes two sizes too small, with holes in the toes to give him more room. In the garden he went barefoot, which I suspected was because he valued his only pair of shoes, which he rinsed out sometimes in the evenings and let them air dry on the balcony.

The family money was scarce, and I learned that the average factory worker's household was taking in what amounted to one hundred US dollars each month, so Solomon's contributions provided bread most weeks, and sometimes milk. Despite this, he seemed to have no real connection with the couple, no comfort or conversation. Cornell left in the mornings for the factory and arrived home after dusk. He and Victorita had late dinners at the small wooden table in the kitchen, and they retired early.

The house was always quiet.

On some mornings I'd find a breadbasket outside my door. By the third or fourth day, I realized that I'd lost track of Pete's timing for his arrival in Brasov, but without a way to contact him, all I could do was wait.

I traveled the town on foot during the days, sometimes ventured off into the hillside and just sat there in solitude with a sandwich or croissant from the market. I found a small currency exchange shop and exchanged more of my American dollars for ron, the new currency of the country. It was beautiful to look at, unlike the money we held in the States, and it fascinated me how nearly all other countries produced art as their currency, often in varying colors.

It seemed appropriate to me that the foundation of a country, the currency of a nation, would be beautifully constructed. It represented the very thing most people spent their lives working for, the one thing each day's work revolved around. The U.S. currency, in comparison, seemed plain and drab with no specific care given to its appearance.

The Romanian notes were romantic, and one paper bill contained images in a soft green and sky blue depicting a beautiful monastery, Gentian flowers, a coat of arms, and a Prince.

*

One day I decided to take advantage of being a foreigner in a new world, and I resolved to eat breakfast, lunch, and dinner at the cafés around town. I walked for miles, touring cobblestone streets, and explored the Basilica Negro, the "Black Church" that had stood since 1834.

I dined on linguini in a thick red sauce at a sidewalk restaurant, finishing off the experience by ordering a glass of dessert wine.

When I returned to the townhouse, I found Solomon in his garden, whistling, and, instead of taking the stairs, I just sat there and watched him. He was a meticulous gardener, and he paid attention to the details of the water and the earth. He bent down to reposition a green sprout that had leaned and tied it to a popsicle stick in the dirt.

Noticing that I was sitting nearby on the wet grass, he stood and grinned.

"You want to work in the soil, Mr. America?"

I grinned back.

"*Nu*," I said, shaking my head. I had picked up a few terms from observing the family and could occasionally reply in Romanian now.

Solomon was a black boy in a white country, and I wondered how he got there. I had seen no other person of color except the gypsies on the street, and their color was lighter, more of an Indian nationality than anything else.

His sole focus was the garden, and it seemed like something he *had wanted* to do, as opposed to something he *had* to do. It seemed like an internal drive, a passion he was destined for, as if to turn the soil and work the land was his only path to connectedness.

"Mrs. B. is making dinner," he said casually.

"Her name is Victorita," I observed. "Why do you call her Mrs. B.?"

Solomon shrugged.

"What work did you do in America?" he asked.

"I sold drugs."

Solomon stood straight, eyes wide.

"Mr. America!"

"Well, not like that," I said, and I laughed. "It wasn't like *that*. I sold psychotropic drugs. Legally."

I saw his blank expression and knew he didn't understand.

"Legal drugs like medicine," I explained. "Drugs for adults or teenagers, mainly. To make them better."

Solomon stared at me.

"To make them better? From what?"

"Well, one of the drugs we sold was a psychotropic drug for ADD, attention deficit disorder, mainly prescribed to teens to help regulate the brain." I found myself slipping into the routine explanation of my work, as if I were on autopilot at a cocktail party back in California. But I could see that he was confused and shifted gears.

"The adolescent brain is wired differently. The prefrontal cortex takes time to develop fully, and that's the area that governs impulses and consequence. Sometimes there are mix ups."

I still couldn't seem to get my point across, and it frustrated me.

"And you sell drugs for that?" he asked.

I shrugged, not knowing what else to say that wouldn't just make it worse.

Solomon stood in the center of the garden and leaned on the tall wooden handle of his plow, waiting for me to continue. When I didn't, he changed the subject.

"You asked me why I call Victorita 'Mrs. B.,'" he said. "You see, adults are all judged by your professions, so I have nicknames for everyone. The world defines people by their work, no? You go somewhere as a man, yet people aren't interested in the man. They ask first, 'what do you do?' As if what you do matters to what you are."

"True," I agreed.

"God sees people as what they are inside, not for what they do. So I have nicknames for people that show the feelings they represent. It's how I see them."

"So what does the 'B' stand for?"

"She's B for bitterness. She has a lifetime of bitterness from years of hanging onto the things people have done to her. And she worries about things that have never even happened."

I stared at the boy curiously.

"Solomon, are you really only ten years old?" I asked after a moment. He seemed much older, like an eighty-year-old in a ten-year-old body. He was an old soul.

"I do not know," he said frankly. "My mother came here from Kenya, and she died in the year she gave birth to me."

"Who did you live with after that?"

"My mother worked as a housekeeper for a family, and they kept me until I was six. I left then and lived on the street with a group of others."

"At six?"

"There are many children who survive on the street," he said.

"And then you came here to live with Victorita and Cornell?"

Solomon nodded. "I work, and they let me live here."

I looked down at the dirt, which was roughly the color of Solomon's skin.

"Why do you call Victorita's husband 'Mr. A.'?" I asked.

"The 'A' is for the anger he has inside."

A small worm burrowed in the dirt beside me.

"So who are you then?" I asked.

Solomon's eyes lit up. "I am joy," the boy said.

I laughed. "You're joy? But you're a beggar! You steal for a living!"

"Ah, but I am a joyful stealer! There you go, defining me for my job. No, I am a joyful stealer!"

We sat for a while, watching the horizon where the sun began to descend over the mountains.

"Then who am I?" I asked.

The boy peered at me, and it seemed as if he looked deep into my soul with the eyes of an ancient teacher.

"You have only been here for seven days," he said, "But your journey is a lot like that of any other man who has been broken by sorrow. A monk, or perhaps a mountain climber facing a difficult ascent that threatens his life. You are like Jesus, who went to the mountain alone after the death of his friend, John the Baptist."

I turned away, and my heart opened up in that moment, as if I could feel it break.

"You," the boy said, "are *sorrow*."

Chapter 8

ADVENTURE

In the morning Solomon was at his garden again. I walked down with a cup of coffee from Mrs. B.'s kitchen and watched him for a while. He was a measure of simplicity—as if simplicity had a face.

"If your seed falls on the path, the birds will eat it," he explained in all seriousness. "If your seed falls on the rocks, it will not grow. If your seed falls on good soil, it produces a crop. It will only grow in good soil."

We talked there for an hour or so before I walked to the café. Along the way, I had time to contemplate him and was surprised at the way I had moved outside of myself and my own turmoil. It was an awareness, more than an awakening.

I ducked into a small shop that served as half butcher, half hardware store and paid 25 ron for a small hand trowel with a red rubber handle. It was a newer, more modern kind like they had in the United States, and I knew he'd love it.

"You're an interesting boy," I told him when I returned. I handed him the trowel, a croissant roll, and a bottle of water. "How did your mother get up here?"

Solomon removed the gifts from the brown paper bag and smiled broadly.

"Thank you Mr. America!"

He dug the trowel into the dirt immediately and set the food and water aside.

"My mother worked for a wealthy Italian family as their housekeeper in Kenya," he said while he worked, "and when they moved here, she moved with them, and then she fell in love."

"Your father is Romanian?"

"I think so. In truth, I do not know."

I wondered how he could personify such joy without knowing where he'd come from. Like a tree with shallow roots reaching into sand, he'd be forever wobbling, wondering. The garden seemed like a metaphor for his life. Did he work in it to feel connected to the earth?

I thought of Pete, then, who had not known either his mother or his father but had now come full circle. He had said he was returning in three days, but many more had passed. I imagined him traveling the countryside and finding an abandoned vineyard or villa he'd decided to buy and renovate, like *Under the Tuscan Sun*. I envisioned him sitting in a sidewalk café, sipping something, chatting up strangers about the ways of the world.

"Tell me your story," the boy said. We stood in the center of the courtyard, surrounded by tall masonry walls painted white. A woman hung sheets and thin towels on a line stretched across a balcony and watched us.

"My story?" I asked.

The boy stood and stared.

"You are locked up, like a vault. That is not good. Tell me your story."

"I don't have a story. Forget about it and explain something for me. How is your English so good?" I asked, changing the subject.

"We all know how to read in this country," he replied. "English is a primary language in the schools. Most of the world knows your language, so it is only you Americans who do not feel the need to understand the other languages of the world."

Mrs. B. passed by on the path and barely nodded at us, and Solomon and I shared a smile. Sure enough, I thought, I'd cure her bitterness.

"*Buna!*" I shouted joyfully, the greeting for hello. "*Buna!*" I said again, this time louder.

Mrs. B. continued on without even a glance in my direction.

Solomon laughed out loud, until he was holding his stomach.

"Oh, Mr. America. Nice try."

I shrugged and broke out laughing myself. Solomon and I stayed there for the longest time.

"We are all teachers," he said finally, "In one way or another. Now the man came to Jesus and said, 'Teacher, what good thing must I do to get eternal life?'"

"You talk in parables," I observed.

"In that verse, the man asked about eternity. Don't we all wonder about the meaning of life? Your destiny is like this garden, and you must water, weed, and repeat."

✳

Later that night I lay in bed and thought about the words Solomon had spoken.

Like the other people I had met recently, he had a mystical quality about him, and I couldn't help but wonder about the meaning of it all. In all my time in suburbia, I had never encountered such magical people. Yet here, on this journey, there was magic all around me, in every word spoken.

Surely back home there had been people with wisdom bottled up inside of them, yet it seemed as if everyone had been too busy working and striving to talk about anything philosophical.

Or could it be that I was too busy striving myself to hear it?

I pondered Peter's concept of angels, and how each person I met along my journey had seemed to know things about me before I even knew them myself. Pete had known that I'd be at the cabin for five days, and he'd been right. His dream about the rainbow on the airplane seemed to be a foreshadowing of the future.

Marilyn, the photographer, had said a few things that no one else could have possibly known.

And then there was Solomon, who seemed like the oldest of old souls. I didn't know how to process it all, but I knew for certain that there was something happening here, something beyond the simple things I could see with my eyes.

I heard a noise outside my room and I got out of bed to find a slip of paper Solomon had slid under the door.

1. zero - zero
2. unu - one
3. doi - two
4. trei - three
5. patru - four
6. cinci - five
7. flase - six
8. flapte - seven
9. opt - eight
10. noua - nine
11. zece - ten

I looked at the list of numbers and said them out loud. Getting back into bed, I repeated them until I fell asleep.

In the morning I awoke with the numbers in my head, smiling at the thought of my littlest teacher. I would make an attempt to learn his language.

Unu, doi, trei, patru . . .

❋

When my feet hit the wood floor at seven in the morning, I was transfixed, stuck in the feeling of *déjà vu*. It was the way the wood floors felt cold and splintered beneath my feet in my old house the day I had slid out of bed alone for the last time.

I froze there in that tiny room in Romania, locked up at the memory of my old life. I had come to escape, but in a flash it was all back. Lacy and Boo. The text message. Anger, bitterness, grief. The stuffed bear, the cars in a tangle of metal.

I glanced out the window again to see the rain falling, spattering the earth and flooding Solomon's garden. He was out in it, frantically moving the soil, digging small narrow trenches to hold the water away from his plants. The rain pelted his dark limbs and it seemed for nothing, but he ignored it and worked anyway.

I ran down and tried to help him, following his lead, using my hands in the dirt. We built a long trench on the outside of the greenery, but, in the end, the hard rain washed his garden away.

He had been growing tomatoes because he'd heard somewhere that his father was a tomato farmer.

Late into the evening we sat in the dirt in what was left of the garden, the mud pooling around us. We were both covered in it, but we didn't care. I saw tears in Solomon's eyes, and my heart felt heavy for him, though his words offered no hint of sadness.

"You have to be willing to let go," he said when I offered my condolences. "There's freedom in the brokenness."

"But the garden was your baby, Solomon," I protested. "I know it was everything to you."

The boy looked up, into the mountains.

He closed his eyes.

"I will have another garden one day."

I went to bed that night and tossed and turned due to the sadness of it all: Pete, Marilyn, Solomon, Lacy, and Boo. Each one was a shard of glass entering my soul, a part of me but not.

A whisper.

I considered my future then. I lay there on the small pillow and thought about my next journey, wondering where it would take me. I had given up on Pete and the hope that he'd come to Brasov. Something had kept him in Italy, and I thought perhaps it was his family. I hoped so, for his sake. Maybe he'd inherited a small house he needed to restore. Maybe he'd met long lost cousins he wanted to reconnect with.

In the days that passed, I spent as much time with Solomon as I could, taking long walks up high into the mountains, surrounded by the tallest trees I'd ever seen. It had been three weeks since I had arrived, the day I found Solomon sitting in the dirt where the garden used to be.

I told him I had made a decision. He spoke before I could tell him what it was.

"You're leaving, Mr. America?"

"Yes, how did you know?"

"You Americans have a saying," he replied. "All good things must come to an end."

I nodded softly. A knot formed in my stomach like a piece of Play-Doh.

"It is not true," he said. "Nothing ends. Even in death, we do not end."

I explained that I felt it was time for me to leave although I admitted I had no idea where I was headed.

He considered my plan to drive to the airport and pick a destination and a plane. There was an old globe in Victorita's parlor. I had looked at it and decided to head to Norway or Holland, two places I'd never been.

"Good," he said. And then, "Remember that there's danger in a divided heart."

"My heart is not divided," I answered.

"Yes," he said, "it is. Half of it wants new life, and half of it wants to shrivel up and die."

I looked at him.

"You're just a kid."

"It is time to water the garden."

"What does that mean?"

The boy smiled. He said nothing and walked away. I knew without words that he meant it was time for me to go, and time for me to think about getting unstuck, time to stop the escape.

But where would I venture to? The journey was far from over, and I couldn't fathom the thought of going back. Back to the States where I'd be nothing more than Mrs. B., filled with bitterness, or Mr. A., a ball of anger.

We traded addresses, and I told him I'd fly him to my country anytime he wanted to come.

"I'll see you one day for sure," he said. "And on that day you will no longer be S for sorrow. I will have to think of a new name."

"Solomon, you're a piece of work."

He looked at me curiously, the phrase lost in translation.

※

The goodbyes with Victorita and Cornell were brief but pleasant. To my surprise, Victorita packed me lunch in a paper bag. There was a muffin wrapped in foil, a bottle of Coca-Cola, and a hard-boiled egg.

The goodbye with Solomon was harder. His face was drawn tight as he took my backpack and insisted on carrying it to the waiting car. He climbed in behind me and said he was making the journey to the airport along with me and would head back to Brasov alone.

"Solomon you can't do that," I said, "It's too far."

"I do it all the time," he said.

And then I remembered who he was. A street-smart adult in a child's body, who had spent many days in the center of Brasov and Bucharest conning money out of tourists.

We rode silently, and Solomon never cracked a smile. We barely spoke, the air between us thick. Eventually

I reached over and put my arm around the boy. His shoulders slumped into me, and he caved into my chest, sobbing.

I was frozen by his emotion.

At the airport we held each other for a long time, and when I let go, he was smiling again. I hoisted the backpack over my shoulder, walked inside, and found the first ticket counter I saw—Alitalia.

"How much is a flight to Amsterdam?" I asked the ticket agent.

"Four hundred fifty-six U.S. dollars," she said.

I gave her my only credit card and held my breath.

Chapter 9

HOLLAND

Amsterdam hit me like a moving train. The airport was thick with human traffic whizzing in all directions, and I decided to avoid the tourists and get out and away from the city as fast as I could.

I rented a car and asked for a map from the car rental agency. The agent outlined the journey to Amersfoort, a small village that dated back to the 17th century. It was a town I'd heard about from my mother, who had traveled there decades earlier on a university exchange program. My brother and I had joked that mom had left an old boyfriend in Holland because she had such fond memories of the tiny town she had lived in for a short time when she was just nineteen.

Amersfoort was situated at the junction of the A1 and A28 motorways. The town was located almost exactly in the center of Holland, near the old town of Utrecht. I clutched the map and keys and slid inside a vehicle smaller than I'd ever been in before, prepared to drive on the left, but surprised to be driving on the right. I made it safely out of the airport through a spider web of canals and waterways as I wound away from the sultry city toward the serene countryside. Flowers blossomed everywhere alongside the road, and the one thing I noticed was an abundance of bicycle traffic, which brought me back to my riding days in college, traversing every inch of the California highways.

Later in life, when Lacy and Boo entered the picture, I switched from road biking to the mountains. Lacy asked me to trade in my Trek street bike with its slick tires for a Gary Fisher mountain bike with fat tires and a knobby tread. I welcomed the change and the chance to ride up into the hills and forest over rocks and roots. The mountain, she reasoned, would be much more forgiving than the traffic on the streets of Orange County.

Besides, she had said, "I'm selfish. I don't want to be a single parent."

In those first years with my new bike, I woke up each Saturday and headed out for a fifteen-minute drive toward a trail, the bike secured tightly on the back of the car. I traded my spandex for heavy canvas bike shorts and felt like a warrior, a man of the mountains riding into the wilderness and away from suburbia. Those weekend mornings were my escape, my release of energy from work and family and the mundane things that threatened to suffocate the adventure out of my life.

Having a new baby was an adventure in itself, but it was a double-sided coin. Something about the permanence of suburbia was smothering, and there was still a small shard of the man I once had been, screaming out for individuality. The division was hard to explain then, and almost unconscious.

Driving into Amersfoort I passed through a town square where hundreds of bikes were locked up, side by side, an awesome sight. I had ridden my bike all over the coast of California, but I had never seen anything like this. A sign near the train station announced a bike rental for sixteen euros a day, and I considered stopping but decided to continue on, in search of a small hotel.

I stopped in a large open public square with shops and flower carts and vendors and left the car at the curb in front of a store, not knowing whether I had parked illegally or not. I followed the walk past a butcher shop, a few restaurants, and some clothing stores until I saw a small bicycle store and ducked inside.

"Hello," I said, embarrassed that I didn't even know the basic words in Dutch.

A woman stood at the register.

"Hallo," she said.

"Hallo," I repeated. "I'd like a rental."

The woman pointed to a photograph on the wall with three types of bikes, then looked over her shoulder and shouted toward the back room.

"Toin!"

Bicycles in mainly silver and black were stacked up on vertical racks on the walls of the tight space, and a rack in the center of the store housed bicycle shorts and Dutch racing team shirts. Black and white photographs of old races, and others of a man on a bike holding a trophy, graced the wall above the register. The woman motioned me to the back, where a man sat at a truing stand, working on a bike. He was wearing a t-shirt printed with *Keistad Fietsen*, the name of the bike shop. His black hair was spiked on top and tipped in blue, and he wore three silver earrings in one ear.

He used a small alignment gauge to adjust the rear derailleur.

"*Hoe gaat het?*" he asked, without looking up. His fingertips were black with grease.

"I, ah . . . uh. Hallo."

"American?"

"*Da*," I replied out of habit, using the Romanian word for yes. "I mean, yes. I want to rent a bike."

The man continued working, testing gears with a special tool.

"How long?" he asked, looking in my direction.

I shrugged. He reached for a small pad of rental forms and pulled the top sheet off, writing the date.

"Name?"

"Jonathan Taylor."

"Beginner, medium, or advance?"

I pondered the question and looked around the shop. Some of the bicycles were foreign to me, but others were Trek and familiar brands I'd seen in the States. I wondered if "beginner" meant cheaper, and if "advanced" meant I'd be paying as much to rent a bicycle as it would cost me to rent a car.

"Advanced," I said, taking the plunge.

A smile traveled slowly across his face.

"You are advance?"

"I used to ride back in America," I said confidently. "A Gary Fisher."

He pointed to a far wall where the rental bikes were racked and then continued working.

"We don't rent those, but we do sell them. Rentals are there. Choose one."

"I see you're using Pedros," I said. "Same tools we use in America." I walked closer, and I noticed for the first time that he was sitting in a wheelchair.

"You know bike tools?" he asked.

I nodded. "I used to work on bikes since I was a kid. Building them with my grandfather." I pulled a chain off of the counter and slid it through my fingers, remembering the bikes we'd fixed for the neighborhood kids when I was young. My grandfather's shop in the back yard was a hub of activity for those who needed brakes adjusted, or a new sprocket put on. He could refurbish a bike from scratch, and, by the time I was twelve, he had taught me to use a disc mount facing tool to work on brakes, and, by the time I was thirteen, I knew the name of every tool, knew how to ensure that disc brakes functioned smoothly, and how to teach other kids to fix basic gear and chain problems.

He held up a tool with a blue handle.

"You know this one?"

"It's a cone wrench. Park Tool Company. Blue handle gives it away."

He shuffled through a row of blue handled tools and held up another.

"This one?" he challenged.

"Tire lever. Lifts the tire from the rim. Come on," I said, grinning. "That's simple. Let's get out of the sandbox."

He looked at me curiously.

"The sandbox. Child's play. A fifth grader would know what a tire lever was."

He reached down to a box on the floor and opened it. He pulled out a tool and held it up.

"This one?"

The tool was distinctly different from the others.

"It's for a cassette," I said.

"Easy guess. But wrong. Another guess?"

I studied it carefully.

"Not sure," I said. "It looks strange."

"It's a wrench for installing or replacing disk brake rotors. It's Dutch. A small company here makes it." He smiled. "I'm Toin," he said, extending his hand.

"What kind of name is that?" I took his hand, and his grip was strong.

"Dutch. 100 percent." He went back to working on the bike, checking the tension cable. "What kind of name is Jonathan?"

"American," I said. "100 percent."

"You want to work?" he asked. "My part-time assistant is away on holiday. We need help."

"Are you serious?" I looked around. The shop had city bikes with rear fenders to keep the rooster spray off the back of your clothes if you were biking your way to work, and then there were professional road racing bikes by various manufacturers. On one wall was a series of mountain bikes with and without suspension, for all sizes and abilities.

I felt the excitement building. I was in my element.

"Yes," I said, nodding. "I'd love to."

I had grown used to following the pull of the universe, the path that had been drawing me through time as if I'd had an invisible compass in the center of my soul. It was that way when I graduated from college and was led to my first job. It felt natural, it was presented quickly, it was a magnetic pull. It was that way when I first met Lacy, as if the compass within me had a magnetic force that led toward her.

Along the way I learned that the Earth, in all of its energetic glory, is a huge magnet with two poles on each end. Without the magnetic pull, a true compass would be useless, and I couldn't help but believe that it was the same way with our lives. Sometimes the most powerful force you can feel is between one space and another in that moment of time between now and the next step. The magnetic pull is everything.

"Where are you staying?" Toin asked.

"I was going to stay at the hotel I passed earlier," I said. "Got any suggestions?"

"The Berg Hotel?"

I nodded.

"It is a great hotel, but it is a conference hotel, and it is very large and expensive, no?"

"I don't know," I said. "Maybe just one night and then I'll find something else."

"You can stay here," Toin offered, and he pointed upstairs. "We have an apartment above the shop. It's three bedrooms, and you can rent it in exchange for work if you'd like."

I thought about the offer.

"Really," he said. "It's very nice."

The woman came out from the back carrying a small brown bag. She placed it on the table beside him.

"Anja will show it to you," he said.

✳

I toured the apartment and in ten minutes Anja convinced me that I might as well stay. She explained their routine and how she and Toin worked in the shop most days and ate out most nights.

Toin had been injured in a career-ending biking accident, Anja said. He had started the bike shop to repair bikes in town, and they were the number one supplier of city bikes. She took me downstairs and told Toin I'd be starting work in the morning.

He glanced at his watch.

"You want to go to the pub with us?" he asked. "We are going now."

"Sure," I said. "Sounds like fun."

"Can I get a hand first?" he asked, motioning me over.

I lifted the bike off of the truing stand. "Where do you want it?"

Toin pointed to a rack high on the wall. I hoisted the bike above my head and stood on my toes to place it gently on the rack.

"Flip it," he said. "Wheels that way." He pointed toward the front of the shop.

I turned the bike around and positioned it.

Toin dried his hands with a wipe and then a towel. He moved the wheels of his chair until he was out and around the front counter, headed to the door.

"We go," he said, and after he had locked the front door, Anja and I followed him down the street and into a lively pub. We passed the bar and moved to a side table, where Toin's wheelchair slid perfectly into it. The barkeep waved a towel at us and in seconds a pitcher of dark ale was delivered. The waitress kissed Toin and Anja both on the cheek and extended her hand to me.

"I'm Nu Nu," she said, and she was so physically striking that I could not reply. Her mouth was small and her cheekbones high, overstated, and she had jet-black hair that fell below her shoulders like a thick cashmere blanket. It was a startling color, like nothing I'd seen on any woman in the United States, a combination of midnight blue and black. She wore sherpa boots and a short denim skirt.

"This is Jon," Anja said, smiling.

I nodded. "Nu Nu? That's a unique name."

"It's a nickname my grandmother gave me. I've just hung onto it."

Nu Nu walked away, and I thought of my girls then. Lacy and Boo were towheads, so platinum in fact that they were showstoppers everywhere we went, whether it was at the town square or the farmers market on Saturday. *Your hair is beautiful!* people would exclaim, asking my wife, *is that your real color?* The latter question frustrated her because of the obvious connection to our child who had the same exact hair.

And if it wasn't her natural color, who cared? In the world we lived in, with processed food, whitener in the toothpaste, and chemicals in the air and water, she reasoned, what was natural anyway?

I drank the glass of ale Toin poured for me and had a flashback to those last sterile days in the hospital, sitting by Lacy's side, and how her hair color had changed. Something about the medication made it turn a darker blonde, almost honey, and it happened within three weeks.

Boo was gone. I had spoken to no one from my former life for months now, but there was no way to avoid the connection to the past. These days I was hit from nowhere with flashbacks, shards of memory flooding in. Lacy in a coma after the accident, the doctors by her side. Lacy uttering small words in the fourth week, emerging out of her cocoon while I moved more and more into mine, a ball of hatred and anger, unable to be the husband I needed to be.

Her mother, her sister, and all of our friends were camped out in the lobby of the sterile hospital, 24/7, and I found myself with no freedom available for my mind and thoughts to grow. I walked out of Lacy's room, and there was always someone there, waiting to offer words that would cure everything that had happened.

The blog someone had set up for donations.

The influx of meals and smells coming into the house.

I was forced to play the role of the devastated father, the caring husband, but it was all false, and, finally, I found that I couldn't do it anymore. Inside of me, there was a hatred that threatened to consume me.

How could she?

The police report was clear. Lacy had been text messaging a girlfriend. Something simple. Something stupid. Just one simple sentence that ended my daughter's life.

Six words.

One thoughtless, careless moment of communication and our entire universe had changed. I couldn't be the caring husband. I *wouldn't* play the game.

Only my brother understood why or how, or that I was even gone. Only my brother was aware enough and outside of himself and his emotions enough to feel what I was feeling.

Mentally, emotionally, and physically even sitting there in the hospital, I had already left. I didn't care about connectedness; I didn't care about a cell phone, about the house or the yard, or the bills.

Two months after the accident, I ran away, while Lacy lay there in a coma in Mission Hospital in Mission Viejo, her life a hinge on the door of tomorrow.

※

"You okay?" Anja asked. "You look like you just lost your best friend."

I felt sick. I had. I couldn't respond.

I drank down the ale and poured another. Someone turned the music up louder, and the human noise at the bar increased a decibel to rise above it, making it difficult to think.

"What brought you here?" she asked.

"I'm having a breakdown."

Toin rolled his eyes. My new friends considered this for a moment.

"Maybe you're not having a breakdown, but a breakthrough," he said. He raised his glass toward mine and we clanked them together. We drank ale after ale, and I told him about my journey from the desert, and the people I'd met along the way. I told him how I had sat in the cabin in the Adirondacks for about three days without doing anything more than looking out the window or getting out of bed to go to the bathroom.

Anja and Toin drank with me and listened and ordered another pitcher when the first one ran dry.

People streamed in and out of the pub, and many walked over and either hugged Toin or waved at him from across the room. Everyone seemed to know him, and when the waitress came with the last pint, I pulled out my credit card, but she refused to take it.

"Toin drinks for free," she said, "and if you're a friend of Toin's you drink free, too."

I was feeling light. The ale had traveled to my head, making my thoughts fuzzy.

"Really?" I said. "I'm liking this friendship already."

A man approached the table with a pen and a photograph and asked Toin to sign it. They spoke in Dutch for a while.

"So are you a rock star, or what?" I asked.

Anja just laughed. "Are you kidding?"

"*Domestique*," Toin said sternly. "You are not a biker. Not a real one, anyway."

"Toin," Anja said. "You've had too much beer."

"He is not an avid biker, or he would know."

"Toin won the greatest Tour in the Netherlands," she explained. "He was a very famous biker, competing in the Tour de France."

I sat and stared at them.

"I'm sorry . . . oh gosh, I'm so sorry." I stared at the wheelchair. "But how . . . "

"Are all Americans like you?" Toin asked.

"What do you mean?"

"Are they all pathetic assholes who sit around and feel sorry for themselves?"

Anja stood up then and walked to the bar.

"I don't feel sorry for myself," I shot back.

"Oh, crime, are you kidding me? You've been sappy since you first walked into the shop. You've sat here for three hours with your face on the floor, lost in your own world."

"You don't know anything about me," I said. "I've lost a lot."

"I know I'm the one in a wheelchair, but you're a way more sorry son of a bitch," he said. I didn't know whether to hit him, or get up and walk away. Once again, I was frozen.

"Old pain is like an anchor," he said. "Useless."

I stared into my glass. The brown liquid swirled. I wondered if I was drinking too much.

"You have to get over it," Toin said, "get back in the game."

"Oh, you're the expert, I suppose. You work in a bike shop and once you were a world-class cyclist? I don't exactly see that as getting back in the game. It's more like giving up."

"I could be bitter myself, you know. I could dwell on the fact that it was *me* who made the mistake that cost me my career, and almost my life. I made one mistake— just one tenth of a second—and now I have to live with it forever."

"You made the mistake that put you in a wheelchair? I thought I heard that you were hit by a car?"

"I was. I was racing and I looked down. I was supposed to keep my eye on the road, but I glanced down at my gears and swerved into a car in our caravan. It was a freak accident actually."

I shook my head in disbelief.

"You're kidding me."

"I had to forgive myself for that one-second lapse of judgment that changed my life. It was so stupid. Years of training out the window."

"How do you deal with it?"

"Not very well," Toin admitted. "But we're all human, and we make errors. We have to move on."

I said nothing. Then I noticed that Anja was back. "So did you boys work things out?" she said wryly.

I exhaled deeply and slumped down in the chair. I looked over at Toin, and he was grinning now.

Our eyes met and we burst out laughing, hysterically.

Chapter 10

EXPECTATIONS

Sometimes you think you know what love is,
what anything is, when really you don't know
anything at all.

— ANONYMOUS

Each morning I stepped into the misty air on the balcony outside of my room and observed the city center. Anja told me that it was still a lot like it had been in the 16th century, when it was built.

The countryside was woody, the landscaping much different and greener than anything I'd seen before. Amersfoort was a city with a country feeling, and on the outskirts were magnificent villages, tiny places where cows, sheep, and farmers lived. But in the center was a firestorm of activity, and in the evenings we'd find our way down to De Hof, an energetic square with terraces full of cafés that overflowed with people.

One night Toin took me to the Lieve Vrouwekerkhof, a square with several bars, and we moved from quieter pubs to bars to nightclubs exploding with techno music and dancers. It was the craziest scene I'd experienced in a long time, and when we left, it was long after any reasonable hour a middle-aged man should encounter.

The next day was ruined, and I stayed inside for most of it, beneath the covers.

✳

In no time at all I became immersed in the culture, feeling more a part of it than anywhere else. The landscape in Amersfoort was mystical.

Nu Nu was studying for her PhD in environmental research at the university in Amsterdam, and she said that the light phenomenon in Amersfoort was a result of an isomere that reflects a strange aura from the sky. There were several theories that artists and historians had debated for years about the Holland light, and filmmakers had even produced a film about it called *Hollands Licht*, which Nu Nu was really into.

Each day the sky would be a unique and distinctly different canvas, and I studied it and took time to glance up no matter what else I was doing. Nu Nu said that the grass in Holland contained more chlorophyll than other parts of the world and reflected light from the clouds that wasn't seen anywhere else.

Some days I'd experience the shadows of dark patches overhead while cycling, and then moments later, I'd encounter an inexplicable patch of light. The sensations were amazing.

※

By the end of the first week, my line in the pub had become infamous, and each time we went there, Nu Nu or someone else would come up to Toin and ask, *So are you famous, or what?* in honor of the American who knew nothing. I laughed it off and drank my ale.

Toin and I became fast friends and were so much alike we could have been brothers.

"What is your trade?" he asked one evening. We'd had two pints already, and I had grown accustomed to the darker ale with its rich texture. Amersfoort had its own beer label, and Toin's bar was famous for its large selection of Dutch and Belgian beers. For some reason the beer tasted so much better in Holland than it had back home. It could suffice as a meal, though the pub offered up great side foods, like a version of shepherd's pie with minced meat and mashed potatoes.

"Excuse me?" I asked. "What do you mean, *trade*?"

"Your trade in America? Your job?"

"I sell drugs. Sold, actually."

Nu Nu stood with a tray balanced in her hand, eyes wide. Their faces grew ashen.

"Not real drugs," I said quickly.

Toin laughed. "Fake drugs?"

Nu Nu placed a round of free shots of liquor on the table.

Toin pondered it for a moment.

"I knew it was not work in a bicycle shop, since you did not know what a chain wear indicator was. Advanced!" He scoffed.

"Very funny."

"I can teach you how to use one," Toin said, " but there are some things I cannot teach."

"Like what?"

"Just like in life, there are things that are basic and things that are art. Building wheels is an art. It takes skill. You have to dish the wheel straight, you have to know how to find the right length spokes. The art is something you have or you do not."

I looked at my new friend and wondered what Solomon would have to say about him. He was a man with a passion so great that it was obvious, in a world of passionless people. He lived the bike, loved bikes, and found fulfillment working on bikes. He had found his passion, while most people spent their lives searching.

"What was it like being a famous cyclist?" I asked, and I was actually dying to know. It was a Thursday night, and the bar and every table overflowed with locals.

"Actually is quite sad sometime," he said in broken English.

"What do you mean?

"I get to live my dream, but at a cost. There is always a sacrifice, and when you are well-known, you do not know who is there because they love you for you, or who is there for what you do or what you represent."

"But isn't all of life that way?

"Yes, but when you are famous, people are drawn to you because it is natural. The association is attractive— the ego of saying you have a famous friend. But with women, it has been a problem."

"What do you mean?

"My last girlfriend before Anja could not stay away from her ex-boyfriend. She met me at the height of my career, and I fell in love. I thought she loved me, too. But as famous as I was, and as big of a life we had, she would always end up back with him. He was a nobody, a mechanic. But in the end, she could not conceal her love for him. Or should I say, her lack of love for me."

"That sucks, man."

"You say what?" he asked.

"It's an American term: *that sucks*. It means something is not good." Toin grinned at that.

"Haven't you ever been out of Holland?" I asked.

He shook his head.

"I have traveled in Europe, but not farther." He looked out into the sea of people and nodded at a man waving his hand in the air. "So tell me about your work with the drugs," he said. "Was it an important drug?"

"Yes," I said. "It was. And it was much more than the drug. My research involved the brain, and my wife's research involved the brain, as well. She was a neurologist, and we were both fascinated with the way the brain works."

"You had a wife?"

"I do," I said, catching myself. "I don't want to talk about it."

Toin raised his hand. "No problem." After a moment I continued.

"I was able to research drugs and their effects on the brain. One of my theories, actually, is that some adults have an undeveloped prefrontal cortex due to trauma or something else that occurred during the critical growth years." I took a long sip of ale and pondered this thought. It was the theory I'd been working on before I left California.

"Other parts of the body can be stunted—such as height—due to improper nutrition or other factors, so it just makes sense that brain development could be stunted in various ways. Sometimes we see adults who have a pattern of inability to judge or decipher consequence. In some of those cases, where there is a consistent lack of judgment, it's my theory that the prefrontal cortex hasn't developed fully."

Toin looked at me. It felt good to talk shop again.

"That's fascinating," he said.

"Really?"

He shook his head. "No."

We both laughed.

"Maybe sometimes we just do stupid things," Toin said. "Maybe it is as simple as that."

"For sure," I said. "For sure."

"You know," he said. "I once had very strong legs. Big legs, like tree trunks. Legs that could power the bike. But now my brain is much stronger. My mind is my greatest asset."

"There are seasons," I said, "for everything."

Toin stared at me. "Wow, Gandhi, that's really profound."

※

After two weeks or so I became accustomed to the routine of working in the bike shop for a half day when Toin needed me and spending the rest of the days touring the small towns in the countryside. Sometimes I'd take the car, but most of the time I'd tour on bike, weaving over streets and waterways exploring, stretching myself in every way.

I wasn't used to riding on slick city streets, and one day I wiped out on the pebbles on the sidewalk in front of the shop and walked in with bloody knees. Toin said nothing, and I was grateful that he let it go.

Later that week I remembered my promise to call Solomon in Romania, and I asked Toin if I could use his phone to make a long-distance call. I rang the number in Brasov and Victorita answered, and in seconds my young friend was on the phone, his voice lit up like a Christmas tree. He asked for my address.

"Are you coming to visit?" I asked, joking.

"No, Mr. America, you have a letter."

"What?"

"A letter has arrived for you."

My heart froze. My mind flashed to the United States, but then I reasoned that no one there knew anything about where I would be because even I hadn't known. I hadn't called anyone, not even my brother.

"From who?" I asked.

"It is from a return address in Italy," Solomon said.

※

I traveled the countryside on a hybrid mountain bike that entire week, weaving in and out of streets, thinking about Pete and his letter. Solomon had said he'd ask Victorita to forward it, and the waiting was difficult.

The scabs on my knees from the wipeout were healing over, and then breaking open in the shower, and then healing over. If I wore pants the friction rubbed against them, opening the wounds again. The aging body was less forgiving, and healing came slower with each passing year.

As a child I could skin my knee and forget about it, and in a week you'd never have known it had happened. Now that I was an adult, the scars remained a lot longer.

※

I made stronger connections in Holland than anywhere on earth, *almost*.

Anja and Toin had been an item for years, and they talked about getting married and the future they'd have, perhaps including children. They were in the process of building a new dream. Toin's dream of being a world-class cyclist had passed, but it didn't seem to stop him from creating exciting new possibilities.

I sat talking with Nu Nu and Anja, and they were like two big sisters who were guiding me. Sometimes Nu Nu would get on her bike and ride out with me into the countryside.

Nu Nu was in the last semester of her PhD, and on the days we rode out into the country, she stopped and gathered flowers, rocks, and specimens of the grass to study. She was always studying, always growing.

One Tuesday morning we rode the bikes to the park and left them alongside a bridge overlooking the water.

We sat down in the damp grass and watched the movement of life. Her English was better than my Dutch, but it was still sketchy, and sometimes she mistook one word for another.

"I read you have a lot of Starbacks," she said. "The place where everyone goes to meet and sit and talk."

"Starbucks?"

"It is the coffee place, no?"

I nodded. "One on every corner, just about. But not like your coffee shops. We don't sell weed in ours."

She smiled. "You like the Starbacks?"

"Not so much," I said. "But my wife couldn't live a morning without it. She would leave the house at exactly ten minutes 'til six just to make sure she had time to stop at Starbucks for her coffee."

"She is without you, in America?"

"Yes."

Nu Nu looked away.

"It must be hard for you," she offered.

"Something like that."

"You have tears in your eyes when you speak of her. It makes you sad?"

"I love her," I said. "But I'm not sure what's going to happen, so it makes me sad to think of her. I don't want to feel sad. I don't want to feel any emotion right now."

"Emotion is okay as long as you realize it is not who you are. Whatever it is that makes you sad or mad, it is nothing. It is just emotion. When we believe our emotions are who we really are, we connect with an identification of the past, instead of the reality of today."

I looked into her eyes and in that moment saw a sea of green. They were large and shaped like almonds. I knew if I looked long enough, I'd see more than just a friend.

"My English is not good," she said. "But how you say, it is to wake up. It is an awakening to live in the *now*. In this moment."

Suddenly I felt sick to my stomach, as if I was being pulled in one direction and would forever ignore the life I used to have. I had been away for nearly two months, so long that I had begun to forget the small things about the life I used to have.

"It's easier to avoid dealing with the pain of the now," I said finally. "Or of the past. I thought we'd be together forever . . . "

Nu Nu rolled her black hair in a ball on top of her head and tied it into a knot.

"Maybe it is time you redefine your definition of forever," she said.

"Meaning what?"

"The house, the wife and kids. That is American dream?" she asked. "Because it seems as if you are mourning the death of a dream and not just death, which is a natural part of life."

"Maybe," I conceded. "But I suppose that's all part of the grieving process." I thought about the dreams that I had created since the moment Lacy and I knew we were pregnant. There were a lot left still that hadn't been realized.

"Maybe life is like a lot of little forevers," Nu Nu said. "Instead of one."

"What do you mean by that?"

"I mean that we consider life to be good if we marry one person and live for twenty years, and the picture is the same. But maybe life is a tapestry, instead. No? It is unpredictable. Maybe life is a series of small stories, instead of just one story."

"I think we should go," I offered.

Chapter 11

LETTING GO

Before I knew it, I found myself acclimating to Holland, the culture, and the language. I could speak in whole sentences about the bikes in the shop now, and my face was covered in new growth. It was an evolution, as if I had shed some part of myself and was moving toward something else.

In general I uttered very few words, went about my work repairing bicycles, and spent some days in the public library, where I could sit with coffee and choose from a wall of books.

There were people who walked into the bike shop and assumed I was Dutch. Many were tourists from other parts of Europe, and some were Asian who couldn't speak English *or* Dutch and just pointed to the signs and talked in Japanese or Chinese. The barriers for language were easily covered by the fact that I seemed so much like a local, looked like one, and had mastered the art of fitting in with merely a few words.

In the essence of escape, I had succeeded. I had escaped the old life and taken on a new one in a new world.

On a Wednesday afternoon, an American came into the shop and asked to rent a bike. He wore a white T-shirt with the logo of my college alma mater, the University of Florida, on the front, and orange Crocs, which were a sure giveaway of his nationality.

"I want to rent a bike," he said.

"*Ik begrijp het niet,*" I replied, staring at him as if I did not understand.

He turned around and waited for his wife, a woman wearing similarly American clothes and shoes. She held a translation dictionary in one hand and a can of soda in the other.

"Can you say the word for bike in Dutch?" he asked her.

We waited while the woman flipped through the book. She pointed to the page and showed it to her husband.

"*Fiets*," he said, struggling. "We would like to rent bicycles."

"*Ja*," I said. Just then Anja walked out from the back.

"May we help you?" she asked, glaring in my direction.

The man exhaled as if stress had been released from his whole body.

"We need to rent bikes," he said for the third time.

Anja took care of their order. She fitted the Americans for two beginner bikes, and they were gone.

"*Goede reis*!" I said, which meant "have a safe journey!"

✳

Later that evening we sat in the pub together, and Anja confronted me about it.

"What is wrong with you?" she said accusingly. "You did not let your fellow countrymen know you were one of them. What, you are Dutch now?"

"I just prefer to stay anonymous."

"Ja," she scoffed. "So you can hide from your life."

＊

That weekend Toin asked me to accompany a group of tourists on a bike outing into the woods and country-side, to see the softer side of the city. It was a tour they did most weekends, with Anja leading along with one of the other bike shop employees, and there was a pre-designated route. The tour would begin at the bike shop and wind away out of the city down the roads, into the greener area.

We started out around eight in the morning, after the last tourist showed up. I had been riding for many weeks now and felt strong, my body awakening before any other part of me, my muscles strengthening and growing.

The tourists followed in single file, with Anja in the back and me taking the lead. After about an hour, a Mini Cooper came from nowhere and nearly side-swiped me, sending me off the side of the road. I swerved over, and my tire slipped off the edge of the pavement the wrong way and sent me into a slide. My fists gripped the handlebars, and I tumbled over the front and slammed hard onto the ground.

Anja rode over and jumped off her bike.

"What happened?" she asked. "Are you okay?"

My heart raced in my chest.

"I almost got killed by that driver is what happened," I said angrily.

"He was nowhere near you," she said.

"What? He almost ran me over!!"

The rest of the tourists sat together in a group, waiting and watching. I picked up the bike and straightened the handlebars, which were bent off to one side. Sweat poured down my forehead.

"He almost killed me," I muttered. After that I rode shakily the rest of the day, unable to relax or enjoy the ride. I put the bike up that night and didn't plan to ride again for a long time.

Days went by without even a consideration to ride, and when Toin asked if I could take a tour out over the weekend, I told him I had other plans.

"I heard you were a *domestique* out there on the tour," he said.

"Domestique?"

"It is the French term for the servant, in a professional bike race."

I knew what it meant.

"I almost got sideswiped," I shot back.

"Fear is an emotional response to danger. Of course, it is natural most of the time. But your fear? Is it natural?"

"I *have* no fear," I countered angrily. Heat rose up the back of my neck, and I felt my face getting flushed.

"What are you fearful of?" he asked, ignoring me.

"I'm not in fear of anything, *dammit*, I was nearly hit by a car!" I pointed at the wheelchair. "You of all people should understand!"

※

That weekend Anja and Toin hosted a party for Toin's forty-fifth birthday, and the tiny apartment was jammed with people. Anja served drinks and Stroopwafels, which were Dutch wafer cookies with caramel inside, and a small birthday cake from the market. Toin was the happiest I'd seen him, surrounded by friends.

"I have someone I'd like to introduce you to," Anja said, tapping my arm. Toin had just poured me their version of a vodka tonic, with Jenever—a Dutch gin. Anja was accompanied by a dark-skinned man in jeans, loafers, and a lightweight cashmere jacket.

"This is Mohammed," she said. "He is from Dubai."

"Hello," I said, shoveling a handful of peanuts in my mouth. "I'm Jonathan."

The man smiled. We stood in the doorway between the kitchen and the family room.

"I have relatives living in your country," he said. "It is nice to meet you. What state are you from?"

"Right now, nowhere," I joked. "But in the United States, I'm originally from California."

"I have family in Texas, but my home is at The Palm, in Dubai. Have you heard of it?"

"Is that the artificial series of islands?"

The man nodded and pulled a photograph from his coat pocket.

"It is in the shape of a palm tree."

"I heard that the majority of the world's construction cranes were over there in Dubai. Is that true?"

"There is a lot of development," he admitted.

We talked for a long time about the state of his country and the state of mine, fascinated with each other's lands. He was on holiday for a week and knew Toin through mutual friends. We talked about our travels and discovered that we'd both spent a lot of time exploring the same places in the world. Mohammed had spent a year working in Romania after he graduated from college.

"Isn't it amazing," he said, "that we can be from continents thousands of miles away and connect here in a small patch of earth in Holland. I suspect we could travel to Israel, or Brazil, and attend a cocktail party or festival and find a connection with others."

"We're all just human in the end," I said.

"Then why do we allow opinions, religion, or politics to divide us? Why do we kill others in favor of our causes? On my honor, I swear, if you do not believe the same way I believe, and you are in trouble, I will still honor you and help you in your darkest hour." His eyes sparkled.

I contemplated my new friend and had a sudden awareness that the level of conversation we were having was not at all the level of conversation I'd had in the past at cocktail parties in Orange County. I couldn't recall ever meeting a man who cared about anything beyond work, his new car, or the most recent vacation to which he and his wife were jetting off.

We certainly never talked about honor.

Mohammed pulled out his business card.

"Give me a call if you'd ever like to come visit," he said. "I own a hotel, and you will not have to pay."

At the end of the evening, with the crowd thinning, I kissed Anja on the cheek and told her I was headed to my room.

"I nearly forgot," she said, holding a finger in the air. "Wait."

She turned for the kitchen and was back in moments with a brown envelope stamped with a lot of international postage.

"For you," she said, handing it over. My name was scrawled across the front, and I ripped it open, anxious to read an update from Pete about what he had discovered in Italy.

The letter inside was handwritten on plain paper.

> Dear Mr. Taylor,
>
> I was instructed to send this to you. Mr. Peter Spinelli had a heart attack in Rome, Italy, and spent time in the hospital here. I was a member of his nursing staff and during his last days, he appeared to get better.
>
> Pete spoke of you, and on the morning before he died, he told me to send this message to you. He wanted to tell you he hopes you found the other side of the rainbow.
>
> Mary Francati, R.N.
> Aurelia Hospital, Roma

I stood there in the hall and read the letter while Anja peered over my shoulder, reading it, too. A hard lump lodged in my throat, and I fought back tears.

"Oh my," Anja said, her hand to her mouth. "Oh no."

I looked down at the paper and the tears flooded out, wetting Pete's last words.

"Is your friend?" she asked.

I nodded and walked down the hall to my room and closed the door.

Yes, I thought. *He was my friend.*

✳

At a café the next day, I ordered a shot of Jack Daniel's and drank it slowly in honor of Pete, the way we used to do on the front porch of the cabin. My stomach was hollow the entire day, and I couldn't go into the bike shop to work because I couldn't face making small talk with customers.

I walked to the library and used the Internet to research Dubai, already planning my next escape and grateful for the mental distraction. I learned about the great construction projects there and the indoor ski area. It was a country being compared to the magical creations of Vegas, with mega hotels that would surpass any found anywhere in the world, including the world's first seven-star property. The landscape was wide and expansive, with giant skyscrapers jutting toward the sky.

At the pub that evening, Toin didn't bring up the letter, so I didn't either.

"I think I'd like to go to Dubai," I told him.

He just looked at me like I was crazy.

We moved out into the street to see a full and florescent moon hanging low in the sky.

"You want to go to another pub?" Toin asked. I looked at his frail figure in the wheelchair. He was thin yet strong, a commanding presence even without the ability to stand. I knew he was only trying to lighten my mood.

"It's one in the morning," I said.

Toin shook his head, as if he were contemplating our next adventure.

"I think I should call my brother," I said finally. "Can I use your phone?"

Toin handed his cell phone over and lit a cigarette, pulling his chair over to the side. I dialed my brother's number and waited.

"Hallo?" I said, in my best Dutch accent.

"John? That you?"

I was silent. Tears backed up in my throat.

"John?"

"Hey, bro," I said. "It's me."

"Where are you?" he asked.

"Halfway across the world. Where are you?"

He laughed. "I'm on a business trip actually. Right now I'm standing in front of the Nike store in Times Square, on my way to a meeting. I can't believe it's you."

I imagined him wearing an expensive suit, ducking into some doorway where the homeless people slept in the bustle of human traffic, straining to hear me across the miles. Loud noises and voices pierced the background.

"She made it," he said.

"What?"

"Lacy made it, John. I thought you'd want to know. She's out of the coma and working in a bookstore in Orange County. The Independent."

I said nothing. It had been two months since I left, and four since the accident. Months had passed since I saw her, but it seemed like it had been years.

"She's been in therapy. She doesn't remember any-thing about the accident."

I felt my whole world unraveling like a ball of string.

"She didn't speak for two weeks after we told her that you and Boo were gone. But she's bouncing back now. She's living in a flat near Laguna." He paused. "The house was too painful for her to go back to, so I helped her pack up her stuff."

"Stop," I said.

"But John . . . "

"Stop!" I shouted. Toin was looking at me now. He reached into the bag on the side of his chair for another cigarette and fired up the lighter, igniting it. The end burned red, glowing in the darkness.

"I just thought you'd want to know . . . " he said. "She's doing fine."

I said nothing. A knot traveled into my heart and remained lodged there. The sounds of car horns pierced the background on the other end of the line.

"This has been devastating for all of us," he said, filling the silence. "I loved Boo like my own . . . " His voice broke. "John, please, just listen to me. It's time to heal, John. It's time for all of us to move on."

"You're telling me to move on?"

"Maybe those weren't the right words," he said. "But what if you changed the expectations of your life?"

We hung up and I felt the heaviness of my old life envelop me, everything and nothing at all wrong with what he had said.

She's doing fine.

I handed Toin his phone.

"I'm leaving in the morning," I announced.

"Where will you go?" he asked.

What if you changed the expectations of your life?

"Dubai," I told him. "I think I'm going to visit Mohammed in Dubai."

Chapter 12

FORGIVENESS

The next morning I woke early enough to catch the brilliant moon shining in through the window, translucent like a big glass ball.

I packed up the last of my belongings, including two cycling shirts Toin had given me. We said our goodbyes, and I told Anja she could drive me to the airport if she promised there'd be no messy farewell. It was easier leaving them than it was Solomon, perhaps because I knew they'd have each other, and I was just another lost soul who wandered into the bike shop one day.

Despite her promise, Anja embraced me tightly in front of the Schiphol Airport in Amsterdam, and we remained there for a while.

"Do the right thing," she said.

I walked into the terminal and started for the Alitalia ticket counter. The monitor listed flights to Dubai International, and I searched for the times as a sea of people passed by. I stepped forward and stood in line, and, when it was my turn, I approached an older ticket agent in a dark green vest.

"Are you going to Los Angeles?" she asked.

I stared at her blankly.

"Excuse me?"

"Do you want to buy a ticket?"

The sign behind her had two flights: one for Dubai and one for Los Angeles. I stared at it, and I turned around and surveyed the line behind me, gathering my thoughts. There were people of many nationalities, some Muslim, some Asian, a few Americans, and most of the others Europeans.

I pulled my passport out of the bag and shoved it across the counter, my heart racing.

"Dubai," I said firmly.

The agent put the passport down beside her keyboard and began typing.

My stomach burned, and the sensation lifted up across the center of my body and settled into my arm. I shifted the backpack uncomfortably, but the pain didn't go away. I felt a heaviness settle in, as if I was going to vomit.

I took a deep breath and closed my eyes.

"Sir?"

I looked down at the floor, resting my forehead on the counter.

"Are you okay, sir?" she asked. Soon there were three agents standing beside her. One walked around and took my bag, holding it for me.

"Los Angeles," I whispered.

"Excuse me, sir?"

Inside I felt an urgency I hadn't felt before. I needed to get home, and if I didn't go now, I wouldn't have the courage to face what I had left behind. It was easier to ignore the loose ends and move forward to a different land. It was easier not to confront the past.

"Los Angeles," I said, almost shouting. "I need to go to California!"

"Are you changing your mind?" she asked, confused. For some reason, which I could not have explained, that made me angry.

"Well, obviously, yes. I am changing my mind. First I said Dubai, now I told you Los Angeles, so that means I have changed my mind."

Another agent wearing a green jacket with the same gold wings on his lapel stepped forward.

"Sir, are you under the influence of something?"

I stared at him.

"No, I'm not," I said, but I knew I sounded agitated.

"You do not have to be rude," he said. He muttered into his walkie-talkie in Dutch and firmly instructed me to step aside.

Within minutes another man approached and asked me to follow him to a room behind the ticket counter. Once there, I complied with every request, even smiling politely and waiting while an overweight airline employee checked my bag. I knew I risked being held there for days if I didn't say the right things.

Once they were done, they brought me out to the counter again where the original agent glared at me and issued a boarding pass.

Seat 31B
Amsterdam–LAX

※

When we touched down in Los Angeles, I used the last of my money to take a cab ride to Orange County, passing the familiar restaurants and places Lacy and I had once spent all of our time. I had lost seventeen pounds and hadn't shaved in months, my face so overgrown that I doubted anyone would recognize me.

I directed the taxi driver through my old neighborhood, and, when we drove past the house, everything seemed in order. I thought about calling my brother and remembered that my Blackberry was sitting in the top drawer in the kitchen beside the toaster. I considered going in to get it, but then remembered how ridiculous that would be, since I hadn't paid the bill in months.

"Keep going," I said, and I directed him to the arts district, asking him to park in front of the gallery beside the bookstore.

"I'll pay you to wait here," I said, and I got out and traveled the sidewalk, walking past the bookstore to the corner and then back again. I imagined Solomon walking the street in Romania and Pete, elated to find the long lost family he'd always longed to know. I imagined Marilyn then, and Conrad, and felt all of their souls inside of me, connected by one single thread that was breathing life into me, giving me courage to move forward.

I got back into the cab and waited.

Moments later the bookstore door opened and a woman stepped out, followed by a man. She had a slight build like Lacy's, but her hair was short. Lacy's had been long, ending just above her waist, and as straight and fine as a Barbie doll's. The girl looked up, nearly straight toward the cab, then laughed at something the man said.

They moved down the sidewalk toward a restaurant on the other side of the street, and I strained to watch.

She walked like Lacy, but her arms were thinner, and muscled. *Could it be?*

I examined the hair, the blunt cut above her shoulders and the darker color. It was auburn, a tint of red and brown. It wasn't like anything she'd ever worn before. She was wearing skinny jeans and a red t-shirt printed with letters across the front in a modern pattern. Some of the letters were large, some small, and all were jumbled in various shapes and sizes and order, the way my thoughts felt now. She wore tall spiked heels, something I'd never seen her in.

My stomach churned. I had expected to feel anger, but I felt a longing instead. I wanted to talk to her, but I had no idea what to say.

"Let's get out of here," I told the driver, when they disappeared into the café. "312 Emerson."

✳

I found the key exactly where I'd hidden it under the ceramic frog in the garden and entered the house through the back. I opened the door slowly, listening for any sign of life, but there was none. I left my backpack by the door and locked it behind me, walking through hallways and into the dark kitchen.

A post office change of address form sat on the counter, and it seemed as if someone had gotten the mail and then forwarded the address so it didn't stack up in the box for the past few months. There was a letter from my mother and father, lying unopened on the granite countertop along with a stack of bills.

I walked over to the drawer and opened it, turning on my Blackberry. It beeped and buzzed for nearly five minutes, sending off voice mail, calendar alerts, and text messages. Someone had paid the bill. I pressed the button and a text message from my brother popped up on the small screen.

Call me when you see this.

Thinking back, it seemed more possible than ever that there would be people who can see into your life like angels, people who seem as if they were sent to you to deliver a message. I thought of all of the people I'd encountered on my journey and wondered about each one of their lives.

Would Marilyn still be alive? There were Toin, Anja, and Solomon. Lacy, Boo, Pete, and all of the people before them on my journey, who had shared their wisdom and love, leaving a little part of themselves. I felt more complete than ever before, the emptiness replaced with a sense of peace—that everything would be okay. I felt that for the first time, I was unhurried, not rushing toward any specific achievement. I'd listen, let my compass guide me, without pushing and hurrying for outcomes, like I had my entire life.

In the past four months I had transformed, so completely.

Who will I be tomorrow?

The answer to that question didn't seem as important as who I was right now.

✳

I wanted to call my brother. I sat there in the chair in the living room, found the remote, and hit the button, only the cable didn't seem to be working. So I put it back down, picked up the Blackberry, and dialed my brother's number.

In seconds he was on the phone, and he sounded elated.

"Jonathan!? Are you back?"

"I am, little brother. I am indeed."

"You sound well," he said. "You at the house?"

I explained to him about my plans to go to Dubai, and how standing there at the airport, something had clicked inside, and I knew my escape was over. I told him about how I'd driven down to the arts district and stared into the bookshop and watched from a distance before I came home. I swore him to secrecy.

"I need time to adapt," I said. "Don't go calling mom and dad.

"Or anyone," I added.

"Are you going to contact Lacy?"

"I saw her today," I said.

"Where?"

"Outside of the bookstore. But I didn't say anything. I just watched her from the curb, turned around, and left."

"You're going to have to confront it eventually," he said.

"What would you do in the same situation? Would you be able to forgive your wife for the same thing? For killing your child?"

My brother exhaled. The line was silent for a long time.

"It's impossible to say," he said slowly. "But there's a lot of forgiveness that has to take place here, Jon. We've all sent text messages, or taken calls while we're on the road. It doesn't make it right. But the other truth is that you left your wife, the woman you vowed to have and to hold through sickness and in health, and you left her in a coma after two months in the hospital.

"Can she forgive you for that?

"Should she?"

I began crying then, softly.

"I don't know. It's all so screwed up. Our life seems lost."

"Not lost, bro. Just in need of repair. I'm here for you. You can put things back together. Lacy needs you right now."

※

We hung up, and I scanned the house, rooted to the chair for a long time, stuck in my memories of them, of the three of us.

Out of habit I scrolled through the phone and the text messages, deleting most. I sat for a long time until my eyes hurt from staring at the screen, and then I walked upstairs and ignored Boo's room entirely, closing the door when I passed by, pushing out any emotions that threatened my new resolve.

I took a shower in the master bathroom. Lacy's toiletries were gone, and all that remained were old bottles of shampoo and conditioner and the bottle of cherry bath bubbles that Boo used to insist we sprinkle into the large round tub on the days she took a bath in there.

I let the water run for thirty minutes, washing it all away. I had a conversation in my head there, with Lacy, imagining it as if it were real, as if she were right there.

"As smart as we were, we were limited by the life in front of us," she said.

"We had a good life," I replied.

"The greatest," she agreed. "But now we have a different one. We have to be willing to accept the things we cannot see. We have to be willing to believe that there's more than this, more than just the life before our eyes. If we don't, what then?"

In that daydream I stared into my wife's eyes and saw hope. For the first time, *hope*.

※

I turned off the water and found a towel in the cupboard. I dried off, found some jeans and a sweatshirt in my old closet, and pulled them on. A light rain fell outside the window. I stared out into it and felt a memory of them come in before casting it away.

Over the course of the brain study research we'd done for pharmaceutical training, I'd learned about the effects of dissociative disorder, which was a process that occurred when someone who'd experienced a trauma disconnected from it completely and had limited memory of it. Sometimes the mind was able to eliminate the memory, so the trauma could never be recalled.

I wished, then, that it would happen to me.

The next day I found the Lexus in the garage, just as I'd left it. I drove for miles, wandering the town aimlessly like a lost tourist, down one street and then the next, my thoughts fragmented.

I drove past the school Lacy and I had carefully chosen for Boo and watched a group of kindergarteners walk across the crosswalk with a safety patrol. I felt my grief then, as I went slipping into what would have been instead of the reality of what was. I saw a little girl in bright yellow rain boots and I looked away, focusing instead on the road ahead.

I drove for miles into town and pulled over in front of the bookstore. I sat and watched then, for a sign of movement, and saw various customers stream in and out of the store.

The memories came clearer now, unlike the robotic feelings I'd had at the beginning of my journey. At five o'clock, I watched what seemed like the last customer leave the bookstore, and a tingling gathered in my stomach.

Opening the car door, I got out and walked up to the door. I pulled on the handle and a bell on the inside clanged. Lacy stood at the counter, facing me. Her short hair curved sharply along the lines of her face at her jawbone.

I stepped forward, time suspended in slow motion. I heard Solomon and Marilyn and Pete and Toin in my head.

Be alive, Jonathan. Old pain is like an anchor. Let it go.

Your destiny is like a garden. You must water, weed, and repeat.

Lacy's mouth opened, but words didn't come. She set the book she'd been holding down on the counter, her slender fingers graceful as always, like those of a pianist.

"I'm back," I said feebly, stating the obvious.

"I knew you would be," she replied.

She walked forward, stepped past, and motioned me to follow her out into the day. We stood on the sidewalk and leaned against the building.

"I've been watching you," I said. "Mustering up the courage. Your hair . . . "

"I changed it," she said, tears appearing in her eyes.

"I'm sorry," I said.

She looked at me with curiosity, tears flowing hard now.

"For?"

"For leaving." We were both crying now.

"Is this pointless?" she asked, anger appearing in her words. "You think you can just waltz back here and talk to me, as if you hadn't left me there dying in the hospital? Is this even worth repairing?" The questions flooded out.

"I just . . . "

"I'm sorry," she said. "I'm sorry.

"I don't know what to say . . . " she continued. "What do you say to the man you married, after you killed his child?"

"Oh Lacy . . . "

"I can't do this," she said, turning away. "You have to go now."

I stood on the sidewalk and watched the woman I'd married walk away, back into the store again. She locked the door and placed the "closed" sign in the window.

Chapter 13

THE TIME IS NOW

There are lies we tell ourselves, and lies we tell others.

In college I had the same roommate for two years, and we lived in a co-ed dorm on campus in the small town of Gainesville, Florida. Throughout that time, my roommate's parents had visited, and he had the kind of mother who made muffins and sent care packages with cookies and chips and everything a college kid could want, each time calling to make sure it had arrived.

One night his mother called and left a message on the answering machine, and I reminded him to call her back. The next day she left a message again and it sounded urgent. When he came back to the dorm a day later, he had a blank look on his face.

His brother had notified him that their mother had died that morning.

I contemplated telling him about that last call, but I deleted it instead. What difference would it have made? It would only remind him of the truth. And the truth was that he never called her much in the first place, and when she did call him, he never called her back because he'd taken her for granted the way we often dismiss the ones we love. That evening he'd been at some girl's house, staying overnight, while his mother lay dying on the floor from a massive stroke.

The truth would have injured him even more.

Sometimes we make decisions like the one I had made, playing God when perhaps we shouldn't. We create realities in our own minds, judging from our own internal beliefs and perspectives. We feel rejected when someone doesn't call us back, when the intention isn't to reject. We feel anger when someone slights us, without considering that he might just be focused inward, on a problem or unsolved thought.

This is how the world operates. Each human is an individual jumble of limiting beliefs and emotions, toppling other humans like a string of dominos. Each one affects the other, and then another, and so on.

Each thought leads to action that leads to a reaction that may even occur thousands of miles away. One word can infect groups and teams and cultures and entire countries, creating ideas—and ideals—that spread like a virus.

There were secrets and lies I wished I could take back, but nothing I wished I could reverse more than the words I heard that day, months earlier.

I'm sorry, Mr. Taylor, your daughter is dead.

I sat in our old house the next day, in shock, thinking about the conversation. Could this ever be repaired? Was our love still in there somewhere, or was I just lying to myself?

I built a fire in our living room fireplace exactly the way Pete would have done it, methodically stacking the logs around the first foundational one, like a teepee.

Once the fire was roaring, I wrote down the memory I most needed to let go of on a sheet of paper and then tossed it into the fire.

I'm sorry, Mr. Taylor, your daughter is dead.

Instead of hiding from myself and my emotions, I decided to try to confront them. The core of the exercise was to create new meaning for a tragedy, redefining it in your mind. If I created a new meaning—instead of hanging on to the old one—I hoped to be able to move forward. The old meaning might remain in my DNA, like a toxin seeping into my blood, year after year until finally I would find I'd been poisoned.

The new meaning wouldn't change the event, but it would change my perspective of it. I needed to address it, redefine it, and move on. It was a symbolic exercise designed to help me let things go.

I decided that my new meaning for the event that day would be that Boo had been here for a short time as a gift for me, and to dwell on the loss of her would diminish the joy her life had brought to me.

To us.

We're not guaranteed anything, you know, Marilyn had said. *Yet we come into this world feeling entitled as if we are. We arrive acting as if we've been handed a manual for life with a certificate that guarantees us a hundred years.*

I wrote a letter to Lacy one morning, sitting at the kitchen table, telling her I that forgave her. I sealed it in an envelope and left it with a young man who was working the counter at the bookstore.

I called my old boss and checked in, just to catch up with the past I'd run away from, and, as we talked about my old friends and colleagues and clients, I was surprised that I felt nothing. No desire to return, no longing to get back in.

One afternoon I went back to the bookstore at closing time and waited for Lacy, having decided to give it one more try. When she emerged, she didn't seem surprised to see me, and we walked.

We sat outside in the bright California sunshine, talking, and this time things were different. It was as if we'd both had time to take a deep breath.

We walked again and talked of our old life, our relationship, our love. How could we ever get them back?

My life flashed across my mind, like a movie reel. Our wedding, my old job, Boo, the career I'd worked so hard to build—how everything that had been lost would have to be reinvented. We talked for a long time, and I was in a space of numbness, like the zone athletes fall into when they're not really conscious of what is, or what is not. In the end, the zone is the space where everything just flows.

It's as if you're wearing blinders, yet moving fluidly toward a dream. I said that I'd watched her walk out of that store, and I asked her how she could be so happy, how she could smile and laugh and conduct her life as if nothing at all had happened.

"And you're a neurologist, Lacy. How can you work here?" I felt no bitterness then, just an evenness I hadn't been able to access before. I remembered Solomon and what he'd said about how we were judged and defined by our jobs, instead of by who we are.

"I'm sorry," I said, catching myself. "What you do isn't who you are."

She looked away.

"I let go of all that," she said quietly. "Who cares anyway? I love, and I remember our little girl, but I had to let go of the tragedy and the trappings of our old life in order to move on. I had to forgive myself." She shifted her balance, hooking her thumbs into the pockets of her jeans. She looked long and lean, three inches taller than I'd seen her before, in the ballet flats she used to wear. In heels she looked more like a model, her legs slender and firm.

"I had to let go of the medical practice," she added. "It's not what I want to do with the rest of my life. I'll die if I sit around and think of Boo all day." She broke down and covered her face with her hands.

I said nothing, taking it all in. After a few minutes she regained her composure and looked at me.

"Think about how we used to live before," she said. "Was that success?"

"Yes," I answered. "We had a great life. We had Boo with us. You were at the height of your career. You had the respect of your peers, and your practice was thriving."

"Always working. Barely passing each other in the house."

"We had to, Lace. We were building a life. That's what it takes."

"Is it really?" A flash of anger rose in her.

I said nothing because I didn't know the answer. Traveling the world, stripped of practically every material thing, made me realize that I was still myself, and the material things had added up to nothing.

"The truth is," she said, before I could respond, "that I've spent the last several weeks thinking about the way we used to live. I've given it a lot of thought and been through a lot of therapy, Jonathan. We were always in motion, never in pause. Never *once* did we stop to take a deep breath and examine the authenticity of our lives."

"Authenticity?" I couldn't believe her words. She certainly didn't sound like the Lacy I knew, the one who couldn't live without her morning Starbucks on the way to work, the one who made lists for every hour and activity of the day. The one who valued intellect and achievement above everything else.

"Some strange things have happened since Boo's death," she said slowly.

"What kind of things?" I asked.

"Well, I was angry at myself for a long time . . . suicidal almost. I didn't see any purpose for continuing. But these strange people came into my life, even when I wasn't listening, or in search of them."

My heart clenched.

I cleared my throat, but the words wouldn't come.

We had traveled the same journey, yet each alone. I thought of Marilyn and Solomon and Pete and Toin and how they all seemed to have been sent into my life for a reason, to deliver a message about the future. Each one was exactly what I needed during that moment, in my darkest hours. Each one was like a mountain guide throwing me a life-saving rope, holding my weight somehow, as I rappelled down the steepest cliff of my life.

"There were moments of extreme sadness and desperation . . . " she said, "as if I'd lost my way and would never find my sense of purpose or direction. But now I'm more centered than ever before, and it's almost as if a sense of forgiveness has settled over me.

"Jon, I've forgiven myself." She looked me in the eyes. "But I wonder if you'll ever be able to forgive me."

I pulled her close and held her as tightly as I could. And as I did so I cried, sobbing into her hair like it was a child's blanket. As my gasping sobs began to subside, she began to speak again.

"We built a life and bought a nice house and had a child and worked all hours of the day and night. But there's more to life than the way we were. If we had really been authentic, we would have stopped to listen, to spend time together, and to really think about the things we wanted."

She pulled away and held me at arms length.

"I loved our life," she said.

I want it back, I thought, as her eyes surveyed the street. I looked at the light surrounding her and the warmth in her eyes, and all of the bitterness and hatred I'd felt melted away.

"But did *you* love our life?" she challenged. "Did you really? Or are you just romanticizing it now?" Her eyes flashed. "I remember many nights when you were traveling on business, and I wouldn't even be able to get you when I called the hotel room. I remember our arguments after that, and how we didn't talk to each other for days."

"Lacy . . ."

She put her hand up.

"Look, I'm not trying to bring up old garbage. I'm just trying to point out that we didn't have a perfect existence. I was drinking a lot, nearly every night. You were traveling a lot. It wasn't perfect. Only Boo was perfect."

I shivered, either from the cold or the memories. I crossed my arms for warmth.

"I miss her," I said. It was the most honest conversation we'd had in years, or perhaps ever.

"I miss her, too," Lacy said. "What do we have without her?"

I shook my head.

"I don't know. We still have each other, don't we?"

"I don't think we can move forward with each other until we're completely honest and authentic. That might mean some soul searching."

"I've searched," I said quickly. "My soul has been searched." And to my surprise, I realized that I meant it. These weren't just words designed to bridge the gap.

"Did you do anything that mattered while you were away?" she asked, although it sounded as if she really didn't want the answer.

A man passed on the street and entered the bookstore, and they nodded a hello.

I reached out for her, touching her hair.

"You cut it," I said.

"I wanted a new beginning. I changed everything."

I drew my hand back.

"Everything?" I thought about the man. Was he . . . ?

"I'm not seeing anyone," she said.

"But you're not wearing your ring."

Lacy glanced at her vacant ring finger and took a deep breath. We had gone to Laguna to pick out those rings, together, from the nicest jewelry store in town.

"I've learned that the things we can't see are far more powerful than the things we can see," she said. "Yet we've all been driven by the things that are there in front of us. All I can say, Jonathan, is that I've started focusing on the unseen, the love, the memories, the relationships."

Lacy reached out and held my hand, and I felt an electric charge travel up my arm as strong as the day we'd first touched. I pulled her toward me and we embraced.

"We will always have Boo," she said. "In our hearts. But if I can let go of the grief enough to live, you can, too. We can still make a life. We need to forgive each other for what we've done, even though there's a part of me that won't ever release the guilt and despair I feel about what I did that day.

"Yet we need to live."

Be alive, Jonathan.

※

I inventoried the things in our old house and was surprised by how numb I felt about it all. The bikes hanging in the garage brought back new memories instead of old ones. Seeing the Trek made me think of Nu Nu instead of my old life. The small backyard only reminded me of the magnificent earth surrounding Pete's cabin and the way I had wandered the land for hours observing the birds, squirrels, and deer.

Lacy and I spent days talking in her flat and at the house we once shared until gradually we could see our lives merging again. Ironically, I had let go. I realized that everything in our lives wasn't exactly what it appeared to be, and that the plan we held in our minds wasn't necessarily the one we would live. We spend decades building, based on an idea of what we think we need to build, and what others have built.

But what if you throw away the plans and build something new?

In the end it was all about forgiveness. I did something I never thought I could do, and it reminded me of others in the world who did things they never imagined they'd do, things they said they could never conceive.

We woke up one night wrapped in each other's arms, and I turned to her in the dark.

"I forgive you," I whispered, and I pulled her close. We stayed there in that cocoon for a long time, Lacy sobbing silently on my shoulder.

"I forgive myself, too," she said softly.

"I love you," I told her.

✳

A month after my return, we placed the house on the market. The market was slow, though, and we spent the next couple of months cutting back foliage and landscaping and preparing it for a new owner. Lacy trimmed the rose bushes and brought me a red bloom, which we kept in a glass on the counter in the kitchen.

We spent nights on the floor by the fire and had dinners on the back porch. We went to one of our old haunts one night, an Italian place in town, and within minutes, we were approached at the table by one of the couples we had known through Lacy's medical practice. It took them time to size us up, and as we sat there, I watched her with her auburn bob, me with my scruffy face, wondering how they'd recognized us at all.

The wife surveyed me cautiously.

"How are you?" she asked, as if she was approaching a fragile piece of china.

"We're great," I announced.

Lacy grinned. She invited them to sit, but they remained standing, like two Greek statues in a museum.

"We can't stay," the husband explained, pointing across the room. "We've got a dinner party in full swing." He was a noted neurosurgeon in Orange County. He wore a dark silk suit that was worth more than everything in my closet.

"What are you doing these days?" the wife asked.

Lacy shrugged. "Doing?" She kept her eyes on mine.

"You know," the woman said. "For work. I noticed your practice was closed."

The woman wore a cream suit with a large necklace, her hair pulled back in a tight bun. She stood with her hands on her hips, and a small, jeweled clutch tucked under her arm. They were old money, a part of the wealthy establishment that had settled there years before all of the nouveau riche had moved in. Her husband's father had been a surgeon, and his father before him. They were well-respected icons in the medical community and high on the social ladder. Their home was perched on a hillside above the ocean, and when Lacy and I had visited, they took us to the garage and showed us their Bentley.

"I'm working in a bookstore," Lacy said confidently. "The Independent. You should come in some time."

The woman stepped back as if she'd been slapped.

"A . . . a . . . bookstore . . . ?" She quickly regained her composure. I remembered the last time we had seen them at a cocktail awards party for the medical industry and the feeling I'd had about them.

It was the same feeling I had now, a feeling of discomfort and struggle to talk about anything of importance, only back then we'd remained in their social circle, attending every event they ever invited us to, living on autopilot.

Maybe this is what Lacy was talking about, I mused. It felt *authentic* to dislike them now, authentic to realize that we didn't need to be friends with someone just because we shared a profession. *What was that anyway?*

Her husband gripped her elbow and nodded toward a large table in the other room—it was filled with sharply dressed men and women.

"We really need to be going," he said. He nodded at both Lacy and me and said it was nice to have seen us.

He didn't ask us to join them.

※

That dinner, though brief and ordinary, was a turning point. It was an encounter with the past, and I could feel my compass shift.

It shifted from the *then* into the *now*, and with it came a feeling of total release, as if everything I'd ever cared about had changed. I no longer felt like we had to network with those people just to stay in their good graces. I no longer cared about the nice cars and the clothes and the cufflinks and the limos. I didn't care about the next rung on the ladder at the company.

My compass had moved, and I told Lacy so a few days later.

"I had to travel the whole world to figure things out, and you figured it all out just by staying here," I said.

She laughed.

"I still haven't figured anything out. It just is what it is."

＊

Our house sold within three months, in one of the worst real estate markets the nation had ever experienced, something I saw as another sure sign that it was time to move on.

Each week we searched for signs and listened.

And the signs came. The sadness was unbearable, and there were reminders of Boo everywhere. It was clear to Lacy and me that we couldn't stay, no matter how close we felt to her in this place. We had a garage sale and sold the contents of the house, garage, and closets. Our families flew in for the weekend to help and camped out on the floor in sleeping bags. My mother cooked large meals for the entire group using two pots we had left out and we ate on paper plates in a circle sitting on a blanket in the empty living room. I felt like a kid again, back to the days we used to picnic with our parents. My brother washed and gassed up the Lexus and readied it for our journey.

Lacy and I had studied a map and picked a handful of states we'd always wanted to go to but had never seen. We decided to pack up and move the rest of our limited belongings to Utah, where we'd find a cabin in the mountains in a remote town that was easy to get in and out of.

Other than that, we had no criteria and no agenda.

It was a new beginning.

※

The first night in our new town, we drove our way up a winding road to discover a romantic mountainside restaurant. We ordered steak and salads and had a nice bottle of wine and talked about the money we'd saved over the years and stuffed away during Lacy's first few years in practice. We made plans right then for our new beginning, and, by the end of dinner, we decided we'd open an adventure travel company, to help other people find themselves.

"What if they're not lost?" I asked.

"Maybe they are, but they don't even know it yet," she countered.

I smiled, knowing that Lacy was right. On my own journey I'd met several people along the way, and I'd discovered that the true meaning of life was to dig deep to find your destiny and your God-given gifts. Only then, would you truly be plugged-in and connected to the world.

It was in this connectedness that we would thrive, prosper, and be energized enough to create and give back to others.

"Sometimes your life doesn't make sense," she said. "Sometimes the decisions we make seem to make themselves, and it's a magnetic pull that you have to follow."

We worked through our new life in Utah, found a cabin on the side of the mountain, and enjoyed being tethered to nothing. Sometimes we cried about missing Boo, but mostly we looked forward and prayed our way through it.

We started the small adventure travel business and trained to take people on mountain climbing and rafting adventures. We took our first round of executives out on a mountain biking trip across the trails, which reminded me of Toin and Anja.

Through it all, the lesson was not to feel as if we had to look back, but to be free to do so. Not to feel the necessity of having to look forward, but to be free to do so.

The ultimate lesson was to be in the present, to thrive and prosper and build whatever our new life would be.

Lacy and I began to plant an organic vegetable garden on weekends, and we talked about how wonderful it would be to live off the land, to be able to use fresh basil and tomatoes on hand-made pizzas. It was a small dream, but a new one.

Nothing seemed to be sprouting, but we continued on, watering, weeding, and repeating the process once more. After a couple of months, Lacy ran into the house, excited by the new birth of a basil bloom. She held it in her hands, toward me

"There's magic in ordinary things," she said.

I imagined Solomon in his garden with giant red tomatoes, working the soil.

AUTHORS' LETTERS

Dear Reader,

Who are you?

Take a moment to write that sentence down in the center of a sheet of paper. Take a day or two to really contemplate it.

The essence of this book is not only our own personal authenticity about who we are and who we desire to be, but also our connectedness to others and the world. Writing this book took a huge emotional toll on me, and I almost didn't think I'd make it. I felt the pain and loss of the whole world inside of me—the loss and joy of generations before.

It was at times unbearable, yet it reminded me that Jonathan's journey is real, for all of us. It represents the peaks and valleys and metaphor of life. It represents the joy that is there for us, if we are willing to find it. We all have a journey.

Make yours matter.

Love,

Tammy Kling

✳

Dear Reader,

We hope you have enjoyed this book and the documentary *The Compass* as much as I enjoyed being a part of the creation of it.

The documentary took me years to coordinate, create, and film from the moment the idea was first conceived. I was surprised to find that it was an emotional journey for me, and there were times I found myself tearing up as I watched our various guests offer their life-changing wisdom on camera. This is not a project designed to create controversy, or make claims to anything. This is simply a project to pass on the love, wisdom, and knowledge of others.

We are partnered with some phenomenal thought leaders who have made it their life's work to help transform lives. I hope their advice and words on these pages will reach into your soul.

John Spencer Ellis

❋

If you would like to contact us and share your personal story about how this book has helped you in your journey, please e-mail us or contact us via our websites or blog. We look forward to connecting with you!

Tammy Kling
www.escapesuburbia.wordpress.com
www.Tkling.com

Dr. John Spencer Ellis
www.JohnSpencerEllis.com
www.TheCompass.tv

READER'S KEY
Life Lessons in the book THE COMPASS

In Chapter 1, Jonathan is hollow. He has suffered a tragedy that has set him off on a journey of self-discovery. It led to an escape, a typical fight-or-flight method of dealing with severe trauma. His wife and child were in a terrible auto accident, and he fled his old life. The insight here for the reader is a sense that tragedy can change your DNA. It can turn you into something that you're not—a hollow and empty shell. You may think you'll turn to family or to friends for support, but, for some, the only reaction to severe stress is escape. These are coping mechanisms we see in society with our friends and loved ones who go through stresses of all kinds. They range from an escape from society into depression (inward escape) to a literal move (outward escape).

LESSON #1: Marilyn, the first character Jonathan meets on his journey, delivers this lesson. She has gone to the desert by choice to escape one last time because she's been diagnosed with a brain tumor. It seems ironic that she has chosen to escape to the desert because she has little life left, while Jonathan has simply escaped life itself, choosing not to live it but just to exist. In a sense, they've both chosen to escape: Marilyn out of choice and Jon out of need. She's dying; he's already dead. She says, "There are no accidents. We may think that there are, but there aren't." The lesson here is about the destiny and course of your life amidst its peaks and valleys. How those we meet were often placed in your life for a reason. Why are you reading this now? Is it an accident, or are you supposed to be reading this for a purpose?

INSIGHTS: In Chapter 1 Marilyn notices a wound on Jon's cheek. We revisit this later in the story as another character makes mention of it. We learn later that this is a wound he received from the aftermath of the car accident, while he was trying to save his family. It eventually becomes a scar, representing the scars we acquire in life.

LESSON #2: Marilyn delivers a central lesson in this book about our perception of control. We all believe we are in complete control, when really we do not know the beginning, the middle, or the end. She says, "Jonathan, none of us knows anything. We think we know, then we don't. The universe has a way of intervening. Of changing you. In the end, you don't know what you're seeking, and you don't know what you'll find." Much of our lives are out of our control. (But we do not believe this! So we strive to erase fear, eliminate the unpredictable, and control outcomes.)

INSIGHT: We hint at Jonathan's inability to forgive, a big problem in his life and future. We see that he is stuck in three stages of grief: sadness, despair, and forgiveness "without any hope for the last."

LESSON #3: In Chapter 2 Marilyn says, "We come into this world feeling entitled, as if we have been handed a manual for life with a certificate for a hundred years." The truth is we all expect to live forever, or live out our hundred, but we aren't guaranteed that. Make the most of each day! Realize that we have no control over our number of years on earth.

INSIGHT: Another insight we give the reader with the introduction of this character is that there is more to life than we can see.

LESSON #4: Jonathan next meets Pete, an old man living in the Adirondacks. Pete teaches Jon that

"We don't always need to get things. Sometimes there's mystery in life, and we just have to embrace the not knowing." This is one of the most difficult lessons for humans to accept, yet the most evolved humans have embraced it as truth and live their lives accordingly.

LESSON #5: In Chapter 4 Pete tells us that "Sometimes it takes a season of brokenness in order to find the true joy and beauty that can lead to transformation." Tragedy is hard to define, but if you look at some of the world's greatest leaders, teachers, and philosophers, their lives have been marked by it.

LESSON #6: This is perhaps the most critical lesson in the book. Pete asks; "How many summers or falls do you have left Jonathan? Maybe twenty? Thirty? There's no time for warring emotions. We must make a decision to be happy despite the death of our dreams. We must be willing to create new ones."

Life is short! Realize your dreams, but also accept the death of a dream that didn't come true or one you need to change, in order to live a new life and create a new dream. Some people are so tied to their old, outdated dreams without giving intentional, conscious thought to whether those dreams still serve them. God has a plan for your life.

INSIGHT: One of the most important things to understand is that people are placed in our lives for a season. Some come, some go, some stay. It's fluid, like a river. Pete is a breath of fresh air because he does not demand anything and does not ask questions. Jonathan really has nothing to give emotionally because he is spent. Sometimes it's important just to be with someone side by side.

LESSON #7: Even though Solomon is just a young boy, he teaches Jonathan many things. He's an old soul, and one of the lessons he teaches us is that we are not what we do, but we are who we are. American society defines most of us by what we do. And we, in turn, define our identities as adults in large part by what we do and what we achieve in our professional lives.

INSIGHT: In Chapter 7 we see Jonathan observing Solomon in his garden. It is at this point we see our main character waking up to the world, emerging from his cocoon of numbness and pain. He is beginning to see others and connect with them. It is this connectedness with the world that will save him. Jonathan could have sunk into depression and isolation and ended his life. Instead he is rising out of it and connecting with those in his path. Slowly, he is regaining his life.

LESSON #8: When Jonathan gets to Holland and meets Toin and Anja, he discovers his first lesson on his own, which is about following your own compass. He thinks "sometimes the most powerful force you can feel is between one space and another in that moment of time between the next step and now." This is where he is in his life right now, but there is value in the "limbo" or "purgatory" moment.

LESSON #9: At the end of the book after Jonathan and Lacy have reconnected, Jonathan discovers another lesson on his own. How can you rebound after a deep valley in your life? How can you reconnect with the world after a tragedy? Jonathan comes to this realization: "In it all the lesson was not to look back, but to be free to. Not to look forward, but to be free to. The ultimate lesson was to be in the present, to thrive and prosper and build whatever a new life would be. Sometimes it's a series of baby steps, one day at a time."

LESSON #10: Finally, on the last page of the story, the final lesson comes from Lacy: In this life, despite the things we cannot control, *there can be magic in ordinary things*. There are times in our lives that we become too inward and introspective, focusing on our errors, our lives, our challenges, and our growth. It becomes a spiral thought pattern, and we get stuck. Bad things happen, and we have to find a way out. Even in the absence of tragedy it's easy to continually quest for self-improvement and achievement; yet sometimes we just need to be still, and let God work in our lives. At the end of the story, Lacy arrives at a place of stillness. *There can be magic in ordinary things.*

AFTERWORD
Words That Will Move Your Compass
and Transform Your Life

Elie Wiesel once said that *we are all connected by pain.*
Wiesel is the Nobel Peace Prize–winning author of the
book *Night,* and he witnessed the murders of his friends
and family in the Nazi concentration camps, yet went on
to talk about it from a survivor's point of view.

We are all connected—by love, by pain, and, sometimes, by major events.

The philosophy that we are all connected is a major
thread within the story of *The Compass.* Each one of us
travels a very specific and unique journey, yet we are all
connected, and, in this connectedness, there is life.

Sharing our wisdom, gifts, and words with the world
can literally save or change a life. A child who has no
mentor can read a book and develop a value system and
beliefs given by the words of a stranger. That child can

grow into a healthy and strong adult who creates a thriving business and life that touches the life of another, and yet another. It's a process of connectedness and sharing that leads to transformation.

Words are the greatest currency we have to empower a life, build up a soul, and create change. Words transform lives, yet some are afraid to give them, fearful of what someone might think, and others are afraid to receive them. They are afraid to risk, yet there is no transformation when you are locked in fear.

Telling someone you love them, talking about the ways in which someone can transform, or sharing the word of God, life lessons, and your own personal wisdom and knowledge are all things that take a great amount of courage. Share the wisdom, as the greats before you have been doing for centuries.

Socrates was a profound thinker who was sentenced to death for his words, yet his words live on today. In the following pages, please find a gift of profound words from some of the world's most powerful thought leaders, most of whom are our partners in the documentary *The Compass.*

"Most people dabble at life and never commit totally to what they're doing, and, as a result, they never really discover what they want to do in life."

—BRIAN TRACY
AUTHOR AND SPEAKER

"To those who have had any kind of trauma in your lives, quit piling up empty yesterdays. The Lord has given you one get-go in the world; let's go out kicking and screaming!"

—JEFF LEWIS
QUADRUPLE AMPUTEE

"If you have a goal that's important enough at a spiritual level, the rest are just details."

—AL SARGEANT
NEURO PSYCHO-EMOTIONAL RESEARCHER

"Life is for living. As you make your goals and dreams, make your move before you're ready."

—LES BROWN
LEADING MOTIVATIONAL SPEAKER

"I think that we have the power as human beings to choose to have the past define us, or we can choose new chapters in our life, and not let the past determine our future."

—LES BROWN
LEADING MOTIVATIONAL SPEAKER

"All real and lasting success takes a long time, and you've got to build the foundation within yourself and become the kind of person who can enjoy the kind of success you want to enjoy."

—BRIAN TRACY
AUTHOR AND SPEAKER

"Visualize it as if it's already happened."

—DEBBIE ALLEN
THE SHAMELESS SUCCESS EXPERT

"We are most powerful when we open the doorway of our heart through gratitude. It's a powerful state."

—DR. JOHN DEMARTINI
PHILOSOPHER

"The most important attitude to hold when moving toward your life goal is to recognize love."

—BRUCE LIPTON
BIOLOGIST

"My greatest success is behind what I fear to do."

—JOE VITALE
METAPHYSICIAN

"Go out and find out what you love. Set a goal, go after it, and stick with it. Chances are you're going to be so much happier doing that than whatever it is you're doing today."

—BURTON ROBERTS
Survivor CAST MEMBER

"Think about being alive. That is magic in itself and the beauty of creation."

—JOHN ASSARAF
ENTREPRENEUR

"The people that you want around you are igniters."

—TIM RALSTON
ENTREPRENEUR

"Nothing that I do ever proves me worthy; nothing that you do will ever prove that you are worthy. We are worthy simply because we are."

— CHARLIE GAY
HUMANITARIAN

"There's a purpose behind every choice we make. If you feel as if you're doing something that's not good for you, be aware, be smart, and make a different choice. It's that simple."

— DR. ROBI LUDWIG
PSYCHOLOGIST AND GUEST HOST
FOR LARRY KING

"The big learning sometimes is in the pause. On the hard days when you're getting thrashed and life is hard, just pause and breathe."

— ERICH SHIFFMANN
YOGA MASTER

"When you start giving, you become a part of a community of givers, and you start attracting people like you. Givers have a much bigger vision because they are here to change the world in a big way."

—MARIE DIAMOND
FENG SHUI MASTER

"You have everything you need inside of you to get what you want. You know what it is that you need. Listen to the voice that's been silenced by the outside noise. I promise you, you'll find the peace and happiness you're after."

—MARILYN TAM
BUSINESS EXECUTIVE AND PHILANTHROPIST

"Feed your faith and your fears will starve to death. Make sure you're not going through life malnourished. We do get into places where we find ourselves mentally, emotionally, and spiritually malnourished. Listen to something positive every day; read something that will nourish your spirit. There is power in the spoken word."

—ONA BROWN
SUCCESS COACH

"Sometimes the best lessons we learn come only after brokenness. People who survive the brokenness of their hearts and souls are often the most interesting and evolved people in the world."

—TAMMY KLING
AUTHOR OF *The Compass* AND
COACH TO THE COACHES

"Happiness means living your life on purpose. We all came to this earth with talents and gifts, and it is only when you give your personal gifts—your contribution to the world, that you are happiest."

—T. HARV EKER
WEALTH STRATEGIST

"Who you become by accomplishing your goals is infinitely more important than what you get by accomplishing your goals. It is never about the goal. And once you get that, you can let go of the attachment to the goal.

You have the spark of greatness in your heart."

—TOPHER MORRISON
PEAK PERFORMANCE COACH

"Happiness is the journey and the perfect place of perfection."

—JERRY CONTI
HUMANITARIAN

"Life is about celebration and joy. It's about allowing your compass to move, and when it moves, seize the moment, to go on a new journey. It's not what you are, but who you are. Home is where your heart is. You could live in a great big home, but if you don't know who you are, you're really not at home."

—PETER MILLER
LITERARY AND FILM MANAGER

"Do it. Get in the game. One step in the right direction is worth a hundred years of thinking about it. There is no right time. Right now is the right time!"

—T. HARV EKER
WEALTH STRATEGIST

"There is nothing on the outside that's going to make you happy, unless you have peace and joy on the inside."

—KELLI CALABRESE

PHYSIOLOGIST

"Are you only happy on the weekends? What if every day was a happy day and just like a weekend to you? Think about living your life as if every day is a weekend."

—TONY JEARY

COACH TO THE WORLD'S TOP CEOS

"Our three basic needs are food, water, and shelter. Yet we neglect our most precious shelter, our own mind and body."

—KELLI ELLIS

DESIGN PSYCHOLOGIST

The feature length documentary

of *The Compass* shares the story of Jonathan, a man who sets out to travel the world on a journey of self-discovery. It is brilliantly combined with the contributions of twenty-three of the world's leading experts on personal development, success, and life transformation making an impact in the world. Some of these experts include T. Harv Eker, John Assaraf, Dr. Joe Vitale, Marie Diamond, Debbie Allen, Brian Tracy, Les Brown, Dr. John Demartini, and Dr. Robi Ludwig.

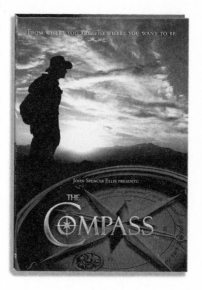

When did your compass move you? To further inspire and motivate you, four storytellers will share their extraordinary journeys through their own life-altering "compass movements" that will guide you to achieve the life you were destined for.

Incredible cinematography brings the beautiful outdoors alive as Jonathan discovers himself, experiences life, and seeks new destinations. The uplifting and inspiring music of Paul Hoffman pulls you into the story, with raw emotion and beauty.

The Compass thoroughly entertains you as it motivates and guides you to reach your goals and live your dreams.

The documentary is available on DVD and can be found in stores everywhere and online at www.TheCompass.tv.